‘Holy crap! What a novel. It’s about a day but also about deep time. About knowing your neighbours and not having the least clue about your neighbours – or, frankly, your loved ones. Keenly observed, superbly crafted, taut, surprising, unflinching, tender, sharply circumscribed, and truly expansive, *Property* is a wonder.’

– Anne Fleming, author of *Curiosities*

‘Kate Cayley’s *Property* is both minutely observed and movingly kaleidoscopic, a meditation on fate, accident, free will, and the elusive and illusive qualities of selfhood. Its questions and hopes – layered into a single day on a single street – are a living, breathing presence.’

– Madeleine Thien, author of *The Book of Records*

‘In this insistently particular and richly detailed portrait of a single street, Kate Cayley has captured the quiet dramas of our private lives, the contested spaces of our neighbourhoods, and the imperfect ways in which we try to understand one another. A wonderful and captivating novel, with a devastating shock at its heart.’

– Jon McGregor, author of *Lean Fall Stand*

Property

Kate Cayley

Coach House Books, Toronto

first edition

Canada Council for the Arts
Conseil des Arts du Canada

Canadä

Published with the generous assistance of the Canada Council for the Arts and the Ontario Arts Council. Coach House Books also acknowledges the support of the Government of Canada through the Canada Book Fund and the Government of Ontario through the Ontario Book Publishing Tax Credit.

LIBRARY AND ARCHIVES CANADA CATALOGUING IN PUBLICATION

Title: Property / Kate Cayley.
Names: Cayley, Kate, author
Identifiers: Canadiana (print) 20250220164 | Canadiana (ebook) 20250220172 | ISBN 9781552455074 (softcover) | ISBN 9781770568679 (EPUB) | ISBN 9781770568662 (PDF)
Subjects: LCGFT: Novels.
Classification: LCC PS8605.A945 P76 2025 | DDC C813/.6—dc23

Property is available as an ebook: ISBN 978 1 77056 867 9 (EPUB), ISBN 978 1 77056 866 2 (PDF)

Purchase of the print version of this book entitles you to a free digital copy. To claim your ebook of this title, please email sales@chbooks.com with proof of purchase. (Coach House Books reserves the right to terminate the free digital download offer at any time.)

For Livia, Tom, and Danny

I will praise as I must
    before the day heaves to its feet

here in my house
    not quite forsaken

– Adam Sol, *Broken Dawn Blessings*

Morning

In the excavated house, there are rats and water.

The rats have lived here as long as the house. Before the house. Before the house, there was water. The water was covered over. The house was built. The water kept on below, and the rats with it.

All the houses in this part of the city are crooked. Foundations cracked, water running beneath.

The water, now uncovered in the basement, flows fast. The rats wash their pretty pink paws.

The men working on the house seal the old tunnels.

The rats dig new ones, unhurriedly. They have all the time in the world.

The rats have memory that crosses generations. More than the raccoons waddling by the train tracks, more than the occasional coyote that eats unwary cats surprised along the bike path in the middle of the night.

The rats are expansive in their generations. They rustle and whisper. They tell.

When the end of the street was a pile of sand and clay, they burrowed underneath it. Every house along the street is fretted with their highways, they flicker through the foundations, wearing them away with their vicious patience, almost as indifferent as the water to whatever stands between them and their path. Later in this day, when someone dies, it will not trouble them. The masonry wall at the front of the basement seeps. The water rises and the rats drink.

Wake up, you fucker, she thought, nudging the dog with her toe. These days, he just slept, mostly, when it was hot. The first hot day, May beginning. Something to talk about. She didn't like it when all he did was sleep. She watched people coming out of their houses, voices rising. Time for a cigarette. They hated that. Kids coming out of houses now. When those kids were younger, he'd come down the porch steps waving his tail, he was younger too, friendly, the mothers pushed their kids at him, she knew why, they wanted to show they didn't think they were better than her. Like she lay awake thinking about them. The smaller girl was afraid of the dog, his long greying jaw. Jumped away when he licked her face, shaking, not sure if she wanted to cry. Now the kids ignored him, he was part of the front steps, part of themselves, like the man who walked all day talking to no one, they didn't think about the man anymore no matter how much the mothers warned. Those mothers thought everyone was out to get their kids. When she was a kid, nobody warned her about anything or anyone. It was fine. Maybe not *fine*, but fine.

The dog looked like an old drunk, Ilya thought, with his red-rimmed eyes and the lines of black around his teeth when he yawned. Ilya parked his truck in front of the fire hydrant, his tools clattering as he heaved them out, preparing to start work on the empty house. He wondered what kind of dog, a mutt, maybe some German shepherd, something big that could turn fierce. He liked dogs, they were one of the things he read about. German shepherds used to be called wolf dogs, used to be thought of as gangster dogs – he pictured a mafia don with a dog like that sleeping at his feet, head lifting hopefully, waiting to be told to bite. But this dog was so old.

Maddy, next door to the empty house, stood on her front steps waving as her husband biked off. Alex didn't see her wave, he took the corner fast, she wished he'd seen her. She was sad at breakfast. He didn't notice, she decided, remembering Alex pushing back his chair, kissing her hair, it was not her fault she couldn't bring herself to answer when he called goodbye from the hall, and then she was sorry and rushed out after him, but he was gone. She stood on the front steps, looking at the young man lifting out his tools, parked illegally across the street. He was thin, jumpy, the muscles standing out in his arms, traced with blunt green tattoos, strange complex knots and crosses and phrases she couldn't read. Nothing was wrong, nothing was wrong. They'd eaten breakfast, and Alex left for work. That was marriage. What did she expect?

The sun was pale gold, the real heat beginning. Another day of drills and hammers and music and the crew shouting at each other (just the young man so far, his shaved head glimmering as the light caught at the bristling fair hair). She glared and smiled as he crossed toward her, and the man, not understanding she was hostile, smiled back and threw his lit cigarette into the road, where, helped by a gust of wind, it spun into a puddle and hissed out. She'd *asked* and *asked* that the men not smoke beside her house, she'd texted the owner, he ignored her, Maddy was sure he must own ten of these ruined houses, trying to fix them quick for a huge profit. Someone should do something, she thought, not sure who or what. She was about to speak as the young man turned away, stepping around the hole yawning at the front door, looking at her over his shoulder as he went inside. She heard the bolt thrust into place, his boots on the stairs. Row houses, thin-walled until recently, now down to a shell on his side. He made her house shake.

In front of the house, the hole. Almost as wide as the door behind it, it yawned at the threshold, making Maddy think of a slapstick comedy. A man like Alex, dressed for work, opening the door, stepping out pompously, then falling into the dark.

The hole led down to the basement. She'd heard them jackhammering, lifting out the earth to make it a living space, not like her basement that you couldn't stand up in. Broken concrete around it, showing sandy yellowish earth streaked with dark clay beneath, growing wet as it went down. Maddy could hear water. The sump pump whirred, stopped again. The hole was only a few feet across, but it was deep. It looked very deep this morning. Twelve feet, Alex had said, frowning, or more. She imagined she could hear rats down there in the dark, scurrying and splashing (could rats swim?) across the length of the wrecked basement, among the scatter of wrecked concrete, half-covered by the water. A canyon full of terrible bones. She would warn Milo again not to go near. She'd caught him last night standing on the plywood they covered the hole with at the end of the day, jumping to feel it give under his feet. Pictured it splintering, Milo vanishing.

On her porch five doors down and across the street, the woman lit another cigarette off the first one, poked her dog's rope with one foot. Her white plastic chair tilted back. She didn't throw her cigarettes into the street, she had a tin can under her chair. And she'd put on her blue velour track suit, dyed her hair dark gold, plucked her eyebrows and filled in the lines. She kept herself up. He was chewing the rope again. She'd get him a new one today, go across the bridge to the hardware store, stop on the way and have a beer with the guys on the porch on the corner of her street, they were already at it, music starting from the fuzzy speakers. 'Gimme Shelter.' Rape, murder. When she was a kid, she'd heard *thought*, not *shot*. It was true: just a thought away. She knew, she knew. She almost saw the Stones once, sometimes she says she did see them. She'd have a beer, maybe two, sing along loudly, and the short-haired woman's pissed-off face would pop up at the living room window of her house across the street. That bitch thought she knew everything, but she'd only lived here ten years, didn't remember when the place where this street curved at the train tracks was just a pile of sand, when almost everyone spoke Portuguese. That woman didn't know shit. The two girls walked by, the junior bitches, pointing at her dog and whispering. They did everything to show that they were friends, but she knew they were on their way out. In a year or two, it would be over, and in ten they would barely think of each other, and in forty they would think of each other again, out of the blue. They didn't know about that yet, thought they knew everything worth knowing, but they didn't know how your whole life came back and knocked the wind out of you.

They stopped on the sidewalk in front of her, whispered. She remembered what that was like, when you wanted everyone to watch you and think about you. They stood, staring at her dog like she wasn't there. The taller one had mean blue eyes, wide open like a cat that wants something. The dog growled and they ran, giggling. Running, they grew younger, colliding at the corner. They made her feel slow and fat, but they would be her someday, joke's on them. She leaned forward to scratch his ears, let him know not to worry about those girls, not to think about them, they were gone.

From her window, Nat watched Clio and Sylvie – her daughter and Maddy's daughter – heading for the schoolyard. Behind her, her wife looked for her keys, lifted the bike pannier down from its brass hook, talking. Nat wasn't listening. She was watching the men on the porch that faced her house, the cooler open, it wasn't even nine. The two old men she thought were brothers, the younger man, probably her age, living harder. Sparse hair, broken teeth, broken veins along his nose and cheeks. That song wasn't appropriate, not for a front porch this early, not with the girls running along the street. She was pretty sure she knew where Frankie's keys were, and was annoyed, Frankie had a sorting system for everything, why couldn't she remember to leave her keys in the little bowl in the hall?

In the house across the street from Maddy's, the very old woman twitched at her curtains. She didn't go outside anymore. But she saw everything. She saw the young man and the woman with her red hair who pretended she didn't like him but looked out of her door again as he descended the ladder to the basement and cursed in a steady stream at all the water. When the light hit just right, she could see into the basement from that hole they'd made where the front steps used to be, but only when the sun reached down in the late afternoon. The very old woman's son, beginning his aimless walk, stopped on the pavement like he thought someone was calling to him. Then he went on, dragging his foot.

The dog falls asleep again. The song ends. The street is briefly quiet.

Nat moved away from her living room window. In the kitchen Frankie was rattling drawers, running her hands behind the set of matching white cylinders they'd bought after the renovation, labelled *rice pasta tea coffee salt sugar* in the spiky typeface of an old newspaper. The expensive final flourishes Frankie had wanted, making the room like a picture of a room, an advertisement marred by the presence of actual people who left socks on the floor or misplaced their keys. It made Nat feel tentative in her own house, trying to tidy away their traces to restore the first calm of that clean vista, wanting to show Frankie how much she had conceded to Frankie's idea of their life. She tidied more frenetically, with more emphasis, when Frankie was just getting back from work and hoping only to sit on the couch or slump at the counter on one of the high stools, looking up to admire the new lights hanging from the ceiling like wide-brimmed hats.

'Did you look in the hall? In your other bag?'

Frankie pushed the containers back into place. 'Yes, obviously,' she said, but went into the hall and opened zippered side panels, the pockets of unpopular jackets.

'I should wake Felix,' Nat said.

'He's twelve,' Frankie said, as if that explained everything.

'So?'

'It's a PA day, let him sleep.'

'He'd sleep all day.'

'No he won't.'

'You don't know that. You'll be at work.'

Frankie paused briefly, went back to the pockets, and Nat found herself angry, following the twitch of Frankie's shoulders into a shrug at Nat, at her more flexible work, her less consequential job, which meant she'd take the girls for a treat while Maddy took Milo to his piano lesson, meant Frankie would competently weave on her bike through the perilous streets, whistling, while Nat was the one tracking the children, the household, the logistics and pitfalls and dangers of a day that Frankie didn't need to concern herself with. Felix could lie in bed staring at his phone, and Frankie thought nothing should be done. It was Nat's job to tie up the loose ends, worry about Felix, wonder what Clio was doing, move through the weekday with no school in a state of irritable suspension, anxious list-making.

'You said it was fine,' Frankie said, now holding up her keys but not calling attention to them, aiming to leave, one hand hovering toward the door handle.

'When?'

'I offered to stay home when you remembered there was a PA day, but I have another harassment meeting, remember? And you said it was fine.'

'I don't remember saying that.'

Silence, in which Nat did remember.

'I'm sorry,' Frankie said, trying to be allowed to go.

'It's just a lot with getting the dinner ready, and those meetings always go late.'

'The dinner was your idea. You don't even like them that much.'

'It's for Clio,' Nat said, changing direction, 'it's something we're doing for Clio.'

'Clio will spend all day with Sylvie anyway. Clio's fine.'

'Clio's fine, Felix is fine, why do you think everything's fine? He's not fine.'

Frankie stopped reaching for the door, her keys hanging from one finger.

'What. What.'

'Nothing. I'm fine.'

'Stop saying that.'

'What do you want me to say?'

Silence.

'I have to go.'

Silence.

'Nat?'

'You're late.'

'Felix is a *kid*. He's just a twelve-year-old kid.'

Nat shrugged as she'd imagined Frankie shrugging, exaggerated and contemptuous, imitating a movement Frankie had not in fact made. Frankie resolutely kissed the corner of Nat's mouth and left, willing to pretend, and Nat, just then, hated that she was willing to pretend. Nat would rather press harder, not knowing how they'd arrived at a standoff about Felix getting up, about the stupid dinner, Frankie was right and this was ordinary, and yet here she was, receiving the kiss without response, as if everything had been revealed as wrong: herself, Frankie, Felix hiding upstairs, Clio somewhere plotting with Sylvie. The wrong places, doing the wrong things.

She touched her mouth as the door clicked shut. The left-hand edge of her mouth, the first place Frankie had kissed her, at a boozy evening for graduate students more than twenty years ago that Nat came to with her girlfriend. Frankie watched her all night, kissed her in the hall as she left. Testing, not lingering. Nat walked unsteadily home, thinking over the offer, if it was an offer, and it made her life seem reckless and exciting. Two children, a mortgage, a marriage, the kiss a private joke, hardened into habit, or conciliation.

In the kitchen, she self-righteously rinsed out Frankie's cup, poured herself another coffee against her better judgment, wanting the flutter of her heart to be partly chemical, to overwhelm her so she could be excused from laughing at herself. The coffee was burnt. She would not pour it down the sink, think of the beans, the workers in the merciless dappled light. *Glory be to God for dappled things,* she thought, and was ashamed, she shouldn't be distracting herself with quotations, she should be thinking of the workers, the beans from who knows where, she'd forgotten where, buying coffee was one of Frankie's errands, from that café on the other side of the bridge, the fancier side, Nat said often, as if she could escape her own good fortune, standing in her new kitchen quoting nineteenth-century poetry.

The dark blue cupboards hurt her eyes, the hard sheen of the paint calling to the bluish tones in the white backsplash. In the showroom Frankie persuaded her the tiles were like soap bubbles, but they were the filmy blue of a cataract, the deep stainless-steel oblong of the sink antiseptic, which was a weird thing to dislike about a sink, but she did.

Nat didn't know how to inhabit this beautiful repellent room. She drank her coffee.

The day focused into a list: check ingredients, simmer the pork in the slow cooker, make the dough and set it to rise, wait for Frankie to text an apology, she would not be the one to begin, make Felix get up – that should be the first thing, make Felix get up because she was right.

'Sweetie! It's time!'

She went back to the kitchen, angry again. She couldn't explain why it was time. When he was small and they went to the park, Clio sleeping in the stroller, he would play alone. Building piles of sand, throwing crabapples at the fence to make a soft brown splatter. Nat would point at the other children: *Look, isn't she in your swim group? Isn't that boy in your class?* Felix, confused, wanting to please her, hating to please her, settling slightly nearer the indicated child, as if this would make Nat leave him alone. She couldn't leave him alone, though his solitude hurt only her. What hurt him was her disappointment. He couldn't understand why it mattered. No one cared as much as she did, not Frankie, not Felix absorbed in his piles of sand. Frankie told her Felix was fine, told her she put too much weight on the present, as if Felix alone with his crabapple game meant Felix alone forever, alone and without the dexterity to change his circumstances because they had not taught him how, they had ignored the signs, and he would become an angry man alone and it would be their fault. Frankie told her to let him be, to let him sleep, to have faith that Felix alone on the playground didn't prophesy his future, without change or surprise. Frankie said these things on her way out of the house; Frankie was not home. Not in the playground either (she was trying to finish her PhD then, Nat had lost heart in hers), watching him, his lips pressed together as the crabapples burst against the bars, his face twisted in heroic imaginary rage, playing out a scene of private carnage that satisfied him. She crept closer, hoping to catch the words. He moved away, muttering. He was friendless, upstairs; she had no idea what he was thinking, pictured his mind growing like a plant unfurling in the dark.

Upstairs in bed, Felix was thinking about dogs. He would never be allowed to have a dog. Frankie said yes, Nat no, Frankie switched to no because a dog was too much work for Nat, she said he'd walk it for a year, maybe two, and then he'd go off into his own plans, and Nat would have to take care of the dog forever. He didn't know what plans she expected him to make.

She called up the stairs in that voice he hated. He sat up and lay back down.

Most people thought a dog really loved you when the dog was actually trying to teach you how to be part of a pack. When a dog follows you around, you might think it loves you, but the dog is upset about the hierarchy because you are doing it wrong. The dog is trying to make you understand. He wondered if the old dog on the smoking woman's porch was still trying to teach her where her place was, or if he'd given up by now. The woman thought the dog loved her. The dog wanted to get everyone to stick to their places. Felix understood.

Nat shouted again that it was time. He sat up again. He didn't know why it was time.

Felix was on the landing, coming down the burnished stairs, his feet bare, the toenails cracked and curling. She couldn't offer to cut them anymore, coaxing him to hold his feet steady over the toilet bowl. Trusting her. He'd slept in his dirty blue shirt again. His fingernails were ragged too, torn.

'Did you sleep okay?'

He lifted the cereal down from the cupboard, got a bowl. Moving ponderously and clumsily, arms and legs hooking chairs and dish-towels. She tried to busy herself at the sink by consulting the recipe she knew by heart (did she have paprika?), wanting to leave him alone, failing. She turned in time for Felix to hug her, which sometimes happened still, though Frankie reminded her not to look for it, not to ask for it. She tried not to hold her breath. He pushed his head into her shoulder, bending his knees so he wasn't taller than she was. A joke between them, like the kiss in the corner of her mouth.

The cereal rustled from the box, milk slopped over the bowl's side. He ate. She looked at her phone to avoid staring at him. Nothing from Frankie. She checked her email, read headlines, averting her eyes as he slurped and chewed. His spoon clinked softly as he placed his bowl by the sink and went back upstairs and nothing was said. The light caught the ring of milk where the bowl had been.

On her front porch, Nat squinted at the sun, dividing the day in her head.

Check with Maddy about the girls and dinner
Make dinner
Wait for Frankie to apologize
Make Felix leave the house
Find Clio and Sylvie

Buy them sweets

Send Sylvie back to Maddy before dinner

Host a dinner party even if it is an affectation to think of it as a dinner party and Frankie is right she doesn't really like them or that's not right either Alex is just bland and she is sorry for Maddy these days but Maddy doesn't like Clio after all that stuff at school as if her own daughter is a fucking saint but Nat has Sylvie's number Sylvie will always be the person who cries to get out of trouble and why shouldn't it be something nice for Clio Nat's mother only made fish sticks with wrinkly frozen peas for greenery and poured too much water into instant mashed potatoes Nat was definitely providing a better childhood oh god she was smug –

Stop it. She set the empty cup on her porch step as she went down. Her house, on the same street as the school, stood at the T-junction with Maddy's short street, which curved where it met the train tracks. On the porch of the house across from Nat's, music blared from the speakers, the three men sitting around the open cooler, nodding in time. Two she thought lived in the house, the third in one of the houses further along Nat's street, toward the crossing for the supermarket, those dingier houses inhabited by people she didn't really know, the houses not yet bought by people like herself. The third man had a scar running along his left cheek, and his drinking seemed more serious. He was young enough that it meant something that he didn't appear to work, perhaps he lived off a married sister, tolerated in an upstairs room, or nominally looked after an old parent, like the walking man with the dragging leg whose mother no longer went outside.

She frowned involuntarily at the men as she passed. Frankie said they meant no harm, the man with the scar and the grey-haired brothers with the twisted arthritic backs and hands of retired construction workers, drinking to ease the pain of injuries they barely remembered. They waved, and for a confused and oddly elated moment she thought they were waving at her, but it was the chain-smoking woman with the dog, arriving, climbing the stairs. The man with the scar handed her a beer as she sat down.

Frankie did not have to listen to their music all day, didn't see the walking man who would, Nat knew, join them at some point. They were the only people he spoke to, except his mother, hiding behind her rigidly pleated curtains in the house across from Maddy's. On his walks, he talked to himself, a heavy gurgle gathering force. She had told the children to stay away from him, just in case. She'd imagined Felix following, riveted by disaster.

She didn't know any of the men's names. Frankie did, Frankie asked.

Frankie had not texted her.

Nat couldn't remember the name of the old woman behind the curtains in the house across from Maddy's either. Maria or Marianna, one was the old woman and one was the woman on the corner by the café she would take Clio and Sylvie to later, the woman with her plastic container of coins and her screeched high note. The girls, fascinated, called her the bird woman, but Nat had overheard someone, probably the woman's caseworker, call her Maria or Marianna, and now Nat could not remember which woman was which.

Maddy's house was just before the curve, beside the in-progress house with the gaping hole at the front. She looked up at the trees standing along the train tracks at the curve, growing against the chain-link fence looped with razor wire. *Glory be to God for dappled things*. What if Felix never left his room. Stop it. Stop thinking.

Behind the curtains, Maria or Marianna watched Nat knock on Maddy's screen door. Nat turned and the woman drew back into her stale darkness. Nat surely made her feel eroded, waiting on Maddy's top step in her jeans and collared shirt, her hair negligently cropped, like she'd successfully sailed past the ritual labours of femaleness as a waste of time.

Maddy appeared, always smiling, beautiful spoiled Milo trailing behind her, wiping his mouth on the hem of her long loose ochre shirt.

'Good morning.'

'Milo, stop, stop that, what are you *doing?* Hi.'

'How are you?'

That young man came out of the house next door, holding a length of baseboard. He laid it across the trestles he'd set up on the sidewalk, as if he owned the sidewalk, you'd have to step into the road to pass, it had been a year of this, sparks arcing, the judder of industrial power tools. Nat didn't know how Maddy stood it. Maddy sighed.

'Oh, I'm fine. Fine. You know. It just goes on and on. And *on*.'

Half-gesture at the young man, who'd picked up a mitre saw. He kept his back to her, determined not to hear.

Nat could see the tattoo on his neck. A lizard? A dragon? He probably believed in the reptilian conspiracy, the deep state, was barely aware he didn't live in America, thought Nat and Frankie were a threat to the future of men, admired Andrew Tate, but what if Felix admired Andrew Tate, she needed to take a look at his search history, she should never have let Felix have a phone, she should take away his phone – Stop it, what was *wrong* with her, stop it.

The young man changed his mind, turned, nodded to them, they nodded back, all hoping for something to say. Nat nearly blushed. (But what if she was right? Stop it.)

'Nice morning,' he said.

'Beautiful,' Nat agreed, opening her hand idiotically at the sun.

Maddy didn't speak, and Nat and the young man waited, it was her turn, nothing happened, the man went back to his work.

Nat touched the edge of Maddy's sleeve above the wrist where the links of her silver bracelet fell over her hand. Maddy's hands were smooth, her nails a little longer than was practical, always clean. Maddy said it kept her sane, knowing that no matter how often she left the house with hardening knobs of egg yolk on her shirt, holes in her socks, she could look at her hands and be comforted. Nat found this grating, since Maddy was preternaturally immaculate. When Milo was an avid crawling baby and Sylvie a demanding and fragile little girl, Maddy's long hair was perfectly combed, a soft pulse of Pre-Raphaelite red, her alert face taut, smooth as a shell.

'Did you text the owner?'

'Twice yesterday. There was so much noise in Milo's bedroom while I was putting him to bed, and I *know* they aren't allowed to work later than seven and I can hear water running through that basement when I'm in my kitchen. You should hear it. They don't even cover the hole into the basement properly. And the smoking! They're smoking inside the house again! He didn't answer the second text.'

'And how's, you know, the rodent situation?' Nat held up her hands like claws, and Maddy laughed.

'Nightmare! I mean, I'm having actual nightmares! I can hear them chewing.'

'Awful.' Nat shook her head, and they both paused, as if waiting for the young man to speak.

The saw whined. Nat and Maddy waited. The end of the board fell.

'Should I still take the girls?'

'Would you? Alex said he could come back early from work, but he didn't figure it out and I don't want to ask now, he gets so grumpy, he never figures out anything in time to help me when school's out. I bet Frankie does.'

Nat smiled noncommittally, thinking of Frankie in the hall with her keys, wanting to go, kissing the corner of Nat's mouth to pretend they were not both angry. She let straight women have their patronizing romantic visions; to contradict Maddy would have felt like letting the side down. Nat was annoyed at the assumed complicity between them, as if they were commiserating housewives, when Nat had an actual job and Maddy turned up occasionally as the first victim in a CBC murder mystery or the harassed yet sassy mother in a commercial for stain remover, grinning at a washing machine in a palatial laundry room.

'What if I take them for a brownie?'

'They would *love* that. What should I bring tonight? Sylvie's really excited. It's so long since we've had dinner with you.'

'Tonight? Anything. Nothing.'

Maddy pouted.

'Fine. Dessert. How about dessert?'

'Oh, perfect. Now I just need to force Milo to sit down and practise for piano!'

Milo howled flamboyantly in protest. Maddy made a half-ironic helpless face, closing the door as the saw started again. Nat stood, not sure why she felt slighted.

The young man blew on the shortened baseboard, pale motes of wood dust flaring in the sunlight. The dragon on the back of his neck had very long teeth. The lettering below it looked Cyrillic to Nat, evoking a fusty childhood aura, mottos on her grandmother's wall that she couldn't read. She was offended by the tattoo, as if it was inflammatory, then rebuked herself. She couldn't read it. It was entirely possible that the tattoo affronted only her taste, not her politics. He went back into the house.

Did she think he couldn't *hear*? He heard everything she said. On the steps, inside the house, talking to her husband at night. Maybe it was noisy. But not like she said. Not all the time.

He wanted to go out again, to see if she'd come back onto the sidewalk. He'd tell her he could hear her. But if he did, she'd stop talking, and he liked listening. Sometimes he'd pause in his work, tools switched off, her voice drifting through the open windows, her terse close-to-tears phone conversations with her husband penetrating the thin walls.

Ilya tried to imagine what the husband was saying, how he was working late and apologizing. Ilya's mother, who watched TV late into the night, would have assumed the husband was having an affair. Ilya knew he didn't have it in him. He was a well-organized small man with a ring of brown curly hair swirling around the beginning tonsure of a bald spot. The unfairness of the universe, that a man like that would have that house, those golden children with their stupid piano practice, that woman with her long red hair and nervous slender hands. He was a twig. Ilya could break him without noticing.

And he didn't smoke in the house anymore. She'd asked, he'd stopped. If the other guys didn't, that wasn't his problem. She acted like he was the problem. He was a good guy. He was respectful. A year working next door and she still treated him like a stranger, surprised he was there. Women like that treated men like servants, Ilya thought, and didn't know what he meant. He didn't know many women, and was embarrassed, and wanted again to talk to her and say he guessed that, secretly, she was not like that, she was only unhappy.

Good luck texting the owner. Ilya could call him ten times, no answer, and then he'd end up shouting into voice mail, standing in the front yard after showing up for a job that needed at least three men and finding himself alone. He liked the feeling of yelling, it was clean and without consequence. He wouldn't be fired, he was too cheap. The owner knew he was lucky to get Ilya, that he wouldn't have him except for the accident.

Today it was okay to be alone, he could work on finishing touches even if it made no sense until the fucking basement was fixed. But he liked accomplishing small tasks, his music echoing in the empty rooms. If the music was loud enough, the woman might come and ask him to turn it down. Sometimes when she asked, she tangled her hair in her hands like she was afraid of him. Ilya wondered if she *was* afraid of him. He didn't know if he minded that. She could be afraid, just a little. Not too much. He was a good guy.

Sometimes at night he turned up the music to drown out the sound of her talking to her husband. Even when he couldn't hear words, he heard sadness in everything she said. How could the husband not see it? But he left early, slipping on his bicycle clips in the yard. The bike was shiny black and silver, fitted with mirrors, bells, panniers of dark red canvas stitched with yellow thread, a thousand dollars those were, probably, and his little knapsack cinched to his back as he rode off, after putting on his helmet with the mirror extending from the wire arm, like he was preparing for an attack from behind. Ilya was sorry for him, leaning over the handlebars of an expensive bike Ilya could lift in one hand, not seeing his wife was unhappy. Ilya wished the husband knew Ilya was sorry for him.

In the front room, Ilya sanded drywall, and the curtains shivered in the house opposite. The old woman watched from behind her curtains, and there was the old woman with the dog. Ilya thought of his mother. Useless old women waiting to die.

The sander hummed, smoothing the dull white walls. They'd got the house down to the studs last year, the original boards dark and pitted, streaked with crumbling orange mould. Ilya, running his hands along the boards, thought about the men who'd sawn them with hand tools, leaning forward, leaning back, the boards transported from the sawmill. The men who'd hammered them into place. No one knew the names of those men. There was no way to know their names, they were visible only in the hammer marks, the square beaten nails.

Ilya had slotted the new hardwood along the subfloor, the glowing boards cut in other countries, carried in the steel hulls of ships. As a child in another country, he'd gone to the docks with his uncle, watched the containers lifted on cranes, the candy colours making him think of toys. The hardwood fed into machines by other nameless people in factories. No one could discover their names. Houses eat names. Everything is eaten.

In bed, Ilya watched videos of snakes ingesting whole animals, the unhinged jaws, the dreadful patience. The house was patient and would eat all trace of Ilya when he left, no one would discover his name. Even assuming anyone wanted to.

All winter he'd worked on the stripped house, snow drifting into his eyes, his fingers frozen. The owner brought in propane heaters, and Ilya stood over them, trying to feel his hands, but the woman next door complained. The thick smell of gas seeped through her walls, gave her children headaches. The husband, warning them he was a lawyer, announced it was illegal to run the heaters indoors. So Ilya froze. Simon laughed at him because he wouldn't wear a hat and had no hair to keep him warm. He'd shaved his head, reading on his phone about shaving your head to show grief, to give up something for your dead.

He liked the new lightness, how he could run a towel briefly over the new-grown stubble on his skull when he showered away the plaster dust at night. He was growing lighter, pared down to his bones.

He'd wanted to burn his hair in the firepit behind his sister's house, but instead he threw it into the trees, walking down the path into the forest. His mother said never let birds make a nest of your hair, he couldn't remember why, witches, binding spells, his mother believed that crap, she believed everything. He threw his hair into the trees and watched it settle, a film over the mossy earth. The birds could have him. Anyone could have him. Let them weave him into nests, pick him to pieces.

He blew on his hands, the drywall dust throwing the raised scars into relief. He'd gripped the rope in time. There was no point thinking about it.

With the sander off, he could hear water from the basement, where they'd jackhammered last fall, lifted earth out from the hole they'd made by the front door, heaving the buckets out of the basement through the opening, where the jagged edges of the outside world showed through, and in the afternoons one shaft of light found its way to the basement's ruined floor. Ilya knew they were destroying the foundation. Cracks appeared in the basement's front wall. The owner ordered them to dig deeper, wanting to add a family room. Tiled walls and floor, half-bathroom, at least fifty grand added to the price. *3 bedroom 2 bathroom fully renovated in sought after up-and-coming west end neighbourhood, close to schools, parks, and grocery stores.*

The heft of those clumps of clay as they dug. Ilya knew they were going too far, that these houses were built on water. At first a greater weight to the shovelled earth, two men, then three to haul up the buckets. A stained piece of plywood covered the hole when they weren't working, and the edges of the hole were crumbling, clots of earth falling down into the dark. Standing puddles welled up, a thin shining layer of water greeting them in the basement each morning. Keep digging, the idiot insisted. The clay melted, slicked their skin grey. At last, he told them to stop. No more mention of a family room. The plumber shook his head.

Ilya heard the sump pump kick in. He could have said something about the water before they started digging out the basement. He knew about the buried creek. But it wasn't his money. It wasn't his house. He'd never have a house. These fuckers had houses and complained about everything like they didn't know they were rich, that fat woman who smoked on her front porch with the old dog had a million dollars because she had a house. The pretty too-narrow streets with their tiny gardens distorted Ilya, he was ungainly and unmoored, as if these rows did not know he existed, an interloper in his truck that was built for wide suburban streets, like the one Ilya lived on, in the basement apartment of a low-rise of glum purplish brick facing a supermarket. He'd chosen the apartment because it was near the highway and the only one he could afford by himself. He'd had roommates before, but since the accident he didn't want to risk being touched, not even a tap on the shoulder, a sleeve brushing his arm. Anything could break him. It was better to live alone, not to have to hear anyone else breathing. He ate at a folding table, congratulating himself on the contrast with his father's cluttered frantic accumulation.

There was an email from Ilya's father; Ilya could see it on his phone. Probably that woman had thrown him out at last, and now he'd have his hand out. He'd be back in the apartment he never got around to finding a subletter for. There were black spots spattered thickly on the basement walls just above the oily broadloom carpet, the bathroom festered with damp, but it was cheap, and nothing was cheap now. If you got something cheap you had to keep it. His father had stayed there on and off since Ilya's mother had thrown his things out into the street, imitating a scene in her head: How a Woman Makes Her Useless Husband Leave. For Ilya the clothes unfolding through the air and his father walking down the stairs, ducking his flung shoes, was part of the upheaval of arriving in Toronto. A place where anything could happen without warning, where he could be dropped off from his ESL class and be told his father didn't live with them anymore.

The basement apartment was furnished with gleanings from his father's sporadic stints on a demolition crew that worked in Rosedale and the Bridle Path. Those were the really rich up there, those shits. His father described to Ilya, with excited contempt, the rooms they were told to strip, making way for new kitchens, bathrooms, bedrooms. The owners sometimes left the furniture, declaring it garbage like the walls and floors and windows. Ilya's father would speculate with the other men on what everything was worth, they'd place bets and look up images on their phones, enraged at the way these people wasted their money, at how easily the owners shook off their possessions as nothing, wanting to change their lives without reference to any past, even their own. The men, heaving everything downstairs and onto tarps laid on the green lawns, fearful that they, hired to throw it out, were also nothing.

Whatever, take any of this shit, the contractor said, so Ilya's father crowded his basement rooms with marble-topped end tables and antique armchairs and watercolour landscapes painted by the dead grandfathers of wealthy strangers, threading his way among his finds like someone lost in the storage vault of a museum.

Ilya didn't blame the woman. Lisa? Lara? Lisa, he thought. Lara was the one before. His father had installed himself with Lisa a year ago, the two of them smoking from morning to night. Ilya had visited them only once. Ilya didn't mind the smell, Lisa's green couch with the tasselled velvet cushions reminded him of his seven-year-old self batting at the smoke from his grandmother's cigarettes, blue from the glowing tip, dull yellow as it streamed from her cracked red mouth, lips pursed to an *o*.

He'd met Lisa only once. He'd arrived at her apartment in the morning and couldn't figure out how to leave. At lunchtime, Lisa's son appeared, the four of them ate, Lisa serving a cat-food-like tuna salad. The son, a little younger than Ilya, was polite and skeptical, obviously wondering why his mother was wasting time on this man who laughed at his own jokes and then winced, complaining about his leg, which Ilya believed had healed long ago, no matter what his father said about going on disability. Lisa seemed nice. She had a job at an office that sold insurance. Ilya knew that Lisa's son should just wait. Given time, she would come to think longingly of an empty bed. And his father would be alone again, which he dreaded. Not knowing, like Ilya, that we are alone anyway.

Ilya knew what his father did not. The birds would have them both.

He enjoyed being proved right about digging out the foundation when the water began rising, like it was showing the solid houses and the people inside that the birds would have them too. These houses were shit, lopsided, built on sand. But he should call the owner again and yell at him that they needed something better than that sheet of plywood covering the hole into the basement. The owner wanted the hole open for now, hoping another plumber could tell them to replace the earth, like that would work (the owner lived in a subdivision in Orangeville and knew nothing). They needed steel, too heavy for a child to lift. Ilya had seen that little boy in the cape from next door kneeling, inquiring into the dark. The boy thought everything belonged to him and he would always be protected and loved. Ilya didn't remember feeling that way for a single moment, but he must have once, wasn't that the point of being a child?

He'd check on the water later. Yesterday, a dead rat bobbed gently against his boot. Brown fur wet, black eyes dulled grey. It must have eaten the poison; rats didn't drown easily. The woman next door said the rats came because Ilya left lunch wrappers on the trash pile in the yard, that's how much she knew about rats. Rats came up when their tunnels were disturbed, so it was Ilya's fault, sure, but not because of a fucking sandwich.

He'd nudged the rat with his toe, wondering why it went in the water to die. He couldn't remember if it was the kind of poison that made them thirsty, so thirsty they would drink water till they burst. He remembered the Pied Piper story his grandmother told him, though she hated German stories, but that one was somehow exempt, too good to waste. The children, the rats in the river, the children following the Piper and vanishing. The quiet of the town, their disbelieving grief. He'd looked it up on his phone and found out it was a garbled inheritance from the Children's Crusade, the soldier of God arriving and persuading the children to follow him. He liked reading about the Crusades, thinking those men must have known real purpose, the crosses on their shields meaning the birds would not have them as they would have Ilya, who believed nothing.

He thought of the woman's red hair tangled in her hands. The sump pump switched off. He'd go outside for a cigarette, hoping to see her. The water flowed through the basement under his feet.

In the schoolyard playground, Clio and Sylvie sat trading handfuls of pebbles by the swings, covering their fingers with fine chalky dust. They'd done this when they were first friends in kindergarten. Sylvie couldn't believe her luck, chosen by Clio, who was so sure of everything. Sitting underneath the swings swapping stones. Staring down anyone who wanted in or wanted to swing. But they were ten and beginning to anticipate endings. Even a year ago they'd be giddy from the day off school, but Clio surveyed the yard with jaded eyes, as if she'd hoped for more, from the day, from Sylvie. This made Sylvie desperate to keep Clio, and Clio faintly curious about what she could make happen. She was not sentimental. Still interested in Sylvie for the moment, sensing new possibilities in Sylvie's apprehensive love.

'Remember that camp counsellor?'

'Which one?'

'With lip piercings.'

Clio nodded, sticking out her lower lip. 'I'm getting a lip piercing when I'm sixteen. And septum.'

'That would be so cool.'

Clio ignored Sylvie's approval, felt her lip, grazing the spot she'd chosen.

'Remember when she told us the Old Woman in the Vinegar Bottle?' Sylvie went on.

'She wants to have nicer and nicer things and then she ends up back in the vinegar bottle.'

'I was scared of it because I thought the bird woman lived in a vinegar bottle.'

'You're scared of everything.'

Sylvie didn't object, wished she hadn't mentioned camp in case Clio wanted to bring up how she'd pissed the bed after the same counsellor told them the story about the Green Ribbon, the young wife with her head rolling on the floor. Sylvie whimpering in the warm wet, thinking it was blood. The beloved counsellor cursed under her breath. Clio was unexpectedly kind, taking Sylvie to the shower, not telling anyone. They had gone back every year, they were going this summer, and Clio never told. The point was that she could.

'We'll see the bird woman today. Your mom is taking us.'

'Oh my God, Nat is driving me *crazy*,' Clio said, reminding Sylvie that she called her mothers by their names, which seemed like part of her liberty. Nat fussed and interfered, but Clio shrugged her off, twisted away, which Sylvie didn't know how to do with her own mother, who was so easy to hurt. You could wound her without noticing, like accidentally tearing a thin sheet of paper, those handmade origami sheets she bought Sylvie that were too good to use, dyed pink and yellow with flecks of gold, the light shining through.

'Maddy's making me crazy too,' Sylvie said, unconvincingly.

'Nah, your mom's always really nice.'

Clio got up, tossed the pebbles over the climber. They rattled down. Sylvie involuntarily covered her head and Clio laughed, so quietly she could deny it.

She stretched her arms over her head, the cropped shirt she'd finally persuaded Nat and Frankie to buy her lifting over her belly. Sylvie wished the persuasion had failed; it had been one of her only advantages, that her mother (her father didn't have opinions on her clothes) let her wear crop tops with rhinestones and flip sequins, that her mother took her to have her ears pierced, but here was Clio suddenly, with gold butterflies in her lobes and *Girls Run the World* sparkling across her chest, where breasts were beginning. Sylvie was losing.

'We need some more stuff for the box,' Clio said, bringing her arms down.

Sylvie got up and sat again when Clio did, quickly enough that Sylvie appeared overeager. Clio dug her hands into the pebbles and threw another handful. The white stones flashed in the morning sun. Sylvie didn't duck this time. She tried to make herself look as bored as Clio looked, the risky boredom of girls on a formless spring day when they are trying to figure out what comes next.

E*veryone is fighting a battle you know nothing about,* Maddy thought, sitting Milo in front of the TV and closing the curtain. Over Bluey's theme, she told Milo for the third time not to open the door for anyone and to ask the man next door for help in an emergency. The man owed her that. And he'd be competent, she knew, decisive. Alex wanted everything explained so he could deliberate on the proper course. She'd be gone twenty minutes. Thirty at most. Stay on the couch. Don't touch the stove. Milo had never tried, and she hesitated at the idea she'd lodged in his head, his sleeve catching in the wispy blue flame. She called out at the door not to eat anything, not even a banana. Couldn't a banana be a plug in the throat, given the right angle?

On the front steps, she waited, hoping the man would come outside. She could hear a sander from the open upstairs window. Maybe if she stood for a minute (able to see Milo through the pane), it would be best. Milo would be drawn into watching, would not get up while she was gone. And the man might come outside.

She turned to look at Milo. If the man came outside, he'd see her in profile, wonder about her enigmatic face bent to the dusty glass.

Milo was completely absorbed now. Even watching television he didn't slacken, his expression never passive. She'd bring him one of those disgusting tubes of pink yogourt. The thought of the oily coil turned her stomach, like the saccharine smell of his toothpaste breathed into her face at bedtime, lying beside him in the stuffed-animal riot of his bed. He liked cutting out paper snowflakes while she read aloud, the sheets prickled with sharp scraps of white paper. And the yogourt tubes couldn't be recycled, Nat told her. If there was any food residue left in the tubes, the whole load would be diverted to landfill. She felt accused every time, but it didn't keep her from buying them. According to Nat, humans would be extinct soon, so what difference did it make? Maddy couldn't see how you could believe that and have children. And she was so tired, she just wanted to bring Milo some yogourt tubes.

When Sylvie was small, Maddy made everything from scratch. Sylvie looked longingly at the lunches of her kindergarten friends, the packages with their brand names in flowing script, pixelated smiling children. Sylvie was convinced she would be found out, cast out, cast away. She refused to know she was loved.

Milo thought everyone loved him. Most people did. Maddy worried that when he discovered love was not his automatic due, it would break him. Unless that never happened to him? Blond, lithe, friendly, good at drawing, good singer, good at sports, gracious as a prince is gracious? Could he maintain that innocence for an entire life? (She believed some men did, but weren't they hateful, monstrous, didn't most people hate them? Didn't she? Did those men actually exist?)

The sander started again. She should stop waiting to see if the man appeared. Shutting the door, she untangled the straps of her cloth bag, wishing Nat could see the bag and approve of it. She crossed at the end of her street so she would pass in front of Nat's house, thinking Nat might see her, which could alleviate the troubling disappointment that the young man had not.

She didn't glance at the men on the porch. Nat's window was empty.

She went on bravely down the length of Nat's street, turned left at the corner toward the supermarket.

Everyone is fighting a battle you know nothing about.

A woman she and Nat knew had posted that on Facebook years ago. That woman in the baby group to which they'd walked together. Meeting, not on purpose yet hopefully, at the end of Maddy's street as Nat was leaving her house, both going to the same place, both a little lonely, pushing their strollers, and their loneliness made them receptive to each other. They would not have been under other circumstances. But Maddy shyly remembered that they'd met ten years earlier. Before baby groups and daughters the same age and houses near each other made a circumstantial and improbable friendship unavoidable. Maddy could tell that Nat didn't remember meeting her, but she pretended to. And Clio and Sylvie flirted so guilelessly from their strollers. Nat dressed Clio in overalls and plain cotton shirts, making Maddy self-conscious about the exquisite embroidered smocks she bought for Sylvie, the hat with the floppy silk bow. Felix was in daycare, Milo not even a thought.

Nat and Maddy found themselves going to parks together. Slowly, they became familiar with the insides of each other's houses, became the person the other texted when late for school pickup. Nat's social circle was older, politically adroit, queer (Maddy stumbled over the word, not sure if she was permitted to use it, but Nat hated *lesbian* and had explained at length why; Maddy forgot), while Maddy's was made up of actors. Family life furnished enough material for conversation, just. Both were at a loss: Nat's friends who had children had not unexpectedly decided to stay home to raise them, Maddy's friends couldn't imagine introducing children into the frenzied dissatisfaction of their lives, temping between auditions, scrambling for voice-overs. Maddy, marrying Alex, saved from that striving, felt exiled rather than saved. Alex came from (and made) what Maddy's mother used to call serious money; Maddy as a child pictured money laid out in solemn rows, somewhere high up, out of her mother's reach.

Having drinks with women she'd known since theatre school, she'd seen the looks pass around the table when she joined in, as if she were not to be taken seriously anymore. She tried not to mind, thinking of her friends living off credit cards and day jobs, hoping for increasingly unlikely luck. But it hurt her (she cried to Alex), the idea that she was frivolous, when she had wanted nothing else in life but to be an actor. She was as serious as they were, even with her vacations and her house and her two children. At that time she was sure she'd go on being an actor. Motherhood was a foggy interlude before she resumed her real life. Her agent said reassuring things. Soon she'd be back onstage, under the hot lights, smelling singed dust and old paint. Or on a set, excited and bored, with someone arranging her hair. Very soon. Alex nodded sympathetically and helped her put away the groceries. There was nothing wrong with him.

Everyone is fighting a battle you know nothing about. Nat had made fun of the post, Maddy remembered; Nat disliked so many things for reasons Maddy didn't understand, which made Nat a dangerous friend.

Maddy secretly loved the post. She tried to believe in the battles she knew nothing about, looking at her neighbours: Nat, the men on the porch, the young man working next door. What were his battles?

Maddy remembered the woman who posted it as especially peevish, cherishing grievances against bus drivers who didn't wait, the truck that splashed her with mud, the waitress who'd asked her to leave her stroller outside the crowded café. Those were the years of complaint, the sleepless years, though Maddy, with a mixture of self-regard and self-command, had complained less than most people she knew, including Nat.

Now she wished she'd complained more. People around her would have listened with a certain degree of sympathy (Sylvie was an inconsolable baby, screaming for hours at a time, Alex away at work). These days she was desperate to give voice to complaint. She had nothing to complain about.

Approaching the supermarket, she imagined sitting down in the middle of the sidewalk and keening. What would happen if she did? The sound of her wail would fade out and the embarrassed passersby would move on and she'd need to figure out what to do next.

It was a sunny morning. She was grateful.

She went through the litany in her head. Her children. Her house. The sun. The spring day. Her marriage, which she probed absently, like the socket of a pulled tooth, but nothing was wrong, nothing was wrong, she was not going to disastrously exit her life like that woman from the café near Milo's piano lesson.

Maddy crossed at the light and doubled back to the supermarket. Nat, even in the stroller days, would dash across three lanes, leaving Maddy behind, timid and correct as her past self at that party where they'd met first, watching Nat hold forth in the centre of the kitchen. Maddy was quiet in those days, studying acting but unlike what people expected an actor to be: calculating their effect, watching themselves. Under her quiet, she was sure of herself. She was an actor, she always would be. The thought of herself at the party with Nat knocked the wind out of Maddy, when she realized that memory was now twenty years old.

Maddy watched other people. She earnestly memorized faces, the curve of a neck, the hunched shoulders, the long scar on the back of the hand, the unconscious flinch or hesitation in the eyes, exaggerated or concealed accent. This made her, several of her professors told her, the real thing. She was merciless, not like those silly girls who wanted only to be admired and loved. She had expected to be the real thing. She didn't smoke, got appropriate amounts of sleep, refused powders and pills, went to the zoo and observed the movements of animals, to the aquarium where she tried to imitate the undulations of fish and anemones. In the morning warm-ups, she staked out her corner on the sprung floor, kept her back to the mirrors, her hair severely braided. Filled with love for everyone in the room, thinking of them as possessing, in their singleness of purpose, a common strength that transcended human pettiness. She'd never felt more open in her life, not sex, not birth. The beauty of the world and her place in it poured through her like light.

She needed to discover that again, she thought, that was what the self-help books advised. She must self-actualize and discover, as though she were a blank space on a map. But that wasn't right, she was crowded and scrawled over. It was that twenty-year-old who had been the blank space. Could she find that again? Breathe. In and out.

At the grocery-store entrance, she paused, breathing. Thinking of the blank space, not the young man working on the house, not Nat's reflexive disapproval, which she thought Maddy didn't notice (why had she said yes to dinner? She could have made an excuse), or Alex taking the corner fast on his bike as she ran outside too late. The young man, seeing her and smiling, lifting the box out of the back of his truck, like his body was pure purpose. The way her acting teachers had told her she was. She liked to think of him as someone who had achieved what she'd missed.

The game was starting. She chose a short stout brown woman pulling a wheeled cart and followed her inside. She would watch this woman and think about becoming her. In the time it took to buy her ingredients, she could do this with at least three people.

As the sliding doors closed, she glanced around her, choosing. The young white man in the hoodie, hunched over his shopping cart, texting as he pushed, staring dolefully at the rows of greens as if he couldn't tell them apart? The older woman, likely Portuguese, in a stained brown duffle coat, heaving a bag of rice from a shelf, her neck spangled with cheap medallions, a profile of St. Christopher, a crucifix, her hands swollen with the bleach she used to scrub her floors? Or that child running, a mucky plastic car in one hand, mouth falling open over his fox teeth? He nearly collided with the woman lifting the rice, leapt around her, his mother pursuing. The old woman took no notice.

Maddy had started the game again. She needed to be ready for the coming work; she would be more than just one of the obscure names in the long list unspooling below her agent's photograph on the agency website. She had so much in her. And she was only forty (for the next two months). She was young. Compared to Nat anyway, who'd been close to forty when Felix was born. Nothing was finished for Maddy. The audition had gone well, the callback better. Her agent would call. She checked her phone. Nothing.

She hadn't told anyone she'd started playing the game again. Her old friends would have pitied her, poor Maddy trying to convince herself she was working, and Alex would have said something encouraging that made Maddy feel like a joke. As for Nat, Maddy had once tried to describe the game to her and why she loved it, and Nat, confusingly, had seemed to think Maddy was wrong to watch a stranger and pretend to be them, saying it sounded unethical. Maddy had stopped talking, obscurely humiliated. They'd looked at each other bleakly, two people who have briefly given up pretending their words mean the same things. Maddy didn't try to justify herself. Maybe there was something wrong with it. Maddy couldn't come up with an answer, except to say that this was what she loved. She understood love was no excuse, or not for Nat anyway.

She'd played this game for twenty-five years, starting at the youth theatre where she took herself to classes every Saturday. You followed someone around the room, in this case a carpeted basement full of teenagers pretending to rush down a street or pace a subway platform. You picked a classmate or, out in the world beyond, a stranger and copied their movement, and with this way in, you became them. Was one shoulder higher than the other? Which foot did they fall on hardest and why? Did they look up or down? Did they angle their hands as they walked, keep their elbows close to their bodies?

The students took turns walking the length of the room, and their classmates had to guess their new identities. Her triumph at fifteen, when everyone yelled the right name before she was halfway across. An older girl who had a boyfriend and went to concerts and protests in support of women's shelters and abortion rights, who seemed to Maddy enviably certain. (Alex was certain; when had she stopped wanting his certainties? She'd once needed them so badly, his promise of a settled life.) Maddy, looking at the girl, discovered where the army surplus bag sewn with sarcastic patches had made her curve her hip even when she was not carrying it, how her left ankle buckled almost imperceptibly. Becoming her, Maddy didn't need to envy her anymore.

Maddy didn't even mind when the boy who chose her showed her as fearful, peering around as if she expected someone to jump out at her, or that some of her classmates laughed, calling out her name. The teacher shook his head, not at the cruelty. He was cruel, though nothing compared to the cruelty she encountered from directors later, the small bullying linger or sneer, the subtle pleasure in degradation. She was often incredulous, remembering what had been done to her and in her presence, as if it had happened to a different person who, when abruptly told to take her clothes off in a rehearsal room full of people, nodded and unbuttoned her dress. There were things she never talked about. There was no way to talk about them without feeling duped, because she'd laughed and braved all of it out, she'd shrugged off her own debasement, and was ashamed.

The teacher shook his head at the boy. *Essence not imitation, are you stupid, why don't you understand?* Maddy was singled out, on the side of art and purpose. She adored the teacher. Now she understood he was dissatisfied, instructing spoiled teenagers (she got a bursary, lived in a small apartment with her mother, was stunned, in scene-study rehearsals, by the size of her classmates' houses) who fleetingly pretended they were actors, showing off in a repurposed classroom. His cruelty was whistling in the dark, seeing the point approaching where his life was fixed. The life he'd wanted wouldn't come to him.

Maybe he hadn't wanted it enough. That was what being an actor meant. You wanted something more than anyone wanted anything, so badly that you were willing to give up everything else. You were rewarded for the naked extremity of your want.

Panicked, she watched an old man arguing with a checkout clerk and thought something was lacking in her. She should have been more focused, more single-minded. Not distracted by children, by marriage, dithering in the supermarket, watching an old man try to persuade a young girl to accept expired coupons.

She followed the stout woman she'd spotted first, trailing behind her in the produce aisles, among the pyramids of spotlit fruit and tangles of misted cilantro and parsley. Was the woman shopping for her family, a meal plan in her head? Or, like Maddy, for a special occasion, a dinner party, something that needed extra attention and indulgence?

The woman's dry black hair was white at the roots. She wore jeans and running shoes, her blue fleece buttoned up to her neck. Maddy conjectured an unexpected flourish under the fleece, a necklace with a blue stone, a silk shirt in purple or dark green. Bought on sale, Maddy thought, as the woman scanned the bins with the yellow Reduced signs in the corner by the hot dog buns and puffy white bread. The woman adjusted her zipper. Maddy saw a coil of silver at her throat. Triumphantly touching the links of her own bracelet, she followed.

She passed an old woman with very blue eyes, masked. She didn't like following masked people, it was too hard to make a story without the whole face. Maddy herself had stayed masked for a long time, and Nat approved at first, then sent her some long articles explaining that the medical literature was inconclusive. Maddy didn't read the articles. Nat read everything and had opinions on everything. Maddy was tired of opinions. She just wanted to look at faces. She'd stayed masked because Alex insisted on it. Maddy suspected dimly that he insisted out of a sense of responsibility to his own social position. He must be seen to do what was right, and Maddy was part of his public face. He was admirable; he was difficult to like, and her difficulty was increasing daily.

What was wrong, nothing was wrong, there was nothing wrong with him, why couldn't she stand anymore his sureness that he knew, always, what was best? What if, when alone, she admitted she couldn't bear him?

She lost sight of the woman in the wheeled cart, thinking of how, when they met, when they married, Alex had anchored her, not only materially (though that was part of it, she knew; people who said money didn't matter had always had it). He allowed her to continue in her state of flux, which he didn't understand was necessary for her if she wanted to keep on being an actor. Her vacillations pained him when he thought of them. He didn't often think of them. That was part of his certainty.

Milo on the couch. She scurried to the baking aisle.

The young man was there, examining brands of vanilla extract, packages of slivered almonds. She would make an almond tart, but she would use whole almonds, blanch and slice them herself. She edged closer to the young man, who was absently patting a package of marshmallows. He looked at his phone again. He was young. How had that happened, that an adult shopping for groceries looked so young she had trouble believing them capable of managing a cart or a list, let alone all the other things? Jobs, degrees, driving, sex, marriage, the question of children. How could such a person look too young for any of that and yet likely be older than she'd been when she moved into Alex's apartment, that stuffy beautifully renovated attic off Queen Street where she grew geraniums on the balcony? Alex was just starting law school. He bought her considerate presents. She thought again of her old friends, the looks around the table in the bar, the humbling sense that she didn't understand, didn't know anymore what it meant to want, compared to her friends, whose husbands were fellow actors or musicians or bartenders or no one.

The young man left the aisle without putting anything into his cart. She considered following him, but Milo was sitting on the couch. It was too late for the young man, the woman with the cart, the old woman lifting the bag of rice. Was it too late for everything? Maddy's eyes filled with tears. That Ed Sheeran song had come on and set her off, Sylvie liked to play it with her door shut, Maddy listened to it after Sylvie left for school, wanting to know what her brittle daughter loved, and sobbed in her kitchen, thinking about growing up and leaving home and missing her children's childhood, her own childhood, the idea of childhood.

She wiped her eyes. The young man was afraid he was not loved. She was loved, she reminded herself, much loved (she recited her blessings, expressed gratitude). Perhaps he was not. Perhaps he was from one of those articles Nat read (worried about Felix), an incel stewing in front of his laptop, angry at all the women who'd wronged him, even women he saw on the street, even Maddy, lovely blameless Maddy, beside him in the baking aisle. His hunch over his cart the hunch at his chair in the basement, typing obscenities, his face immobile in the soft glow from the screen. She imitated his slump over her own cart, staring intently at the icing sugar, trying to see as he saw.

Everyone is fighting a battle you know nothing about. But she couldn't remember what the young man looked like, his face transformed into the face of the young man working next door, with his scalp dusted white with plaster, throwing his cigarette into the street.

She moved away quickly, letting herself begin crying again, overwhelmed by the largesse on the shelves, by the song about growing older, the rows of candied fruit gleaming, the opulence of everything, and she would stop thinking about the young man with his bristled hair growing in again now, she would put everything she saw into her cart, bring all of it home to her children. Sugar cubes and bottled cherries, jumbo boxes of cereal, vegetables of course, unblemished and magically abundant. Nat was always thinking of the pickers and the packers, the truckers on the long treacherous roads, but Maddy didn't see the point, what difference did it make to think of them?

Maddy could think only of people she could see (the young man, the tattoos girding his arms). Nat was wrong in her predictions of food shortages, that they would soon be greeted by bare beige metal dotted with a few cans of cat food. Maddy knew there was a wrongness to these overloaded shelves, full of things people couldn't afford, but she went on crying luxuriously, thinking grateful thoughts.

Her children.

Alex (there was nothing wrong with him, she was just tired).

Gratitude, gratitude. Let in the light.

She looked at her phone. Nothing.

Her agent would call. The audition had gone well, and the callback better. A mother with a missing daughter in a post-industrial town with secrets. A wonderful long scene where the mother broke down howling in the middle of a council meeting, embarrassing the corrupt mayor. Another scene where she ate instant noodles alone in front of the TV and said caustic things to the empty air.

Maddy looked down at her hands. She'd grow her nails, then gnaw them ragged, modelling herself on women she'd seen in the town near Alex's family cottage, she'd follow those women through the supermarket, not the one her in-laws usually shopped at. Alex's mother shopped at the boutique butcher shop and the organic fruit stand near the docks and had the rest of her groceries delivered and tipped well. Maddy would make herself haggard and prematurely aged. She was full of want.

Her agent would call today. Everything would be different.

Maddy thought of other women her own age, former actors who taught yoga classes, coached corporate executives in the art of public speaking, and they claimed fulfillment, but Maddy knew these things were consolations and she didn't want to be consoled. Alex sometimes asked her, with devastating tact, what she meant to do next. Milo was in school, he was not an excuse for her days; she might have listed the household tasks Alex didn't notice, but he did notice, he was conscientious about noticing (there was nothing wrong with him). She wanted to become a small-town woman with a missing daughter. That was the point of her life.

She checked her phone again, crying. She should have been more focused, more like her friends who'd had no children, or only one, later in life, carefully calibrated to not wreck their chances. The thought of Milo not existing made her hurry. His sleeve in the blue flame.

The child with the toy car clutched to his chest ran into her legs. He'd eaten a chocolate bar since she'd seen him last, the chocolate smear elongating his mouth.

'Where's your person, sweetie?'

(Nat said *person*, never *mother*; Maddy had trained herself, wondered if Nat noticed.)

He looked blank. She wondered if he didn't speak English, or didn't speak.

'Can I help you find them?'

He took her hand. She left her cart and walked him up and down the aisles, looking for a frantic woman. She saw her at the same time as the woman saw them and skidded along the concrete floor, she pulled the boy away from Maddy and strapped him into her cart without saying thank you. Maddy had wanted a moment with the woman, sympathizing about the lurch in your stomach, turning to find your child gone, entertaining ruin until the child is spotted by the row of plastic cars. The woman didn't turn back.

The child whispered a secret into his hand.

Maddy would surprise Milo with the toy car she'd refused to buy him last time. He was so sweet later, so contrite, tracing the bruise he'd raised on her ankle, kicking and screaming as she dragged him out. She wasn't rewarding bad behaviour, just giving him an unanticipated happiness, she wanted to give him that while it was still possible for her to give it. The green car with the orange thunderbolt on the hood, the silver wheels like new coins under the gloss of the plastic sheath.

Ilya rubbed the scars on his hands, the white lines like the slashed roots in the earth when they dug out the basement. Grind of the lighter, flare, first drag. He'd stepped onto the curb, he was a good guy, would she notice? Was she home?

He saw the boy through the window, watching the screen. A shape outlined behind the sheer curtain. The boy saw him and pretended not to.

Ilya liked smoking inside. He smoked in his apartment. When he went to live with his sister last year after the accident, she didn't let him smoke inside. It had been only three months since the men fell from the scaffold, leaving Ilya dangling ten storeys in the air, Ellie should have let him smoke anywhere he wanted.

He wished he could sleep.

He went to stay with Ellie after the lawyer cautioned him against the appearance of coping, told stories of private investigators hired by companies to catch claimants on their one good day, when they'd successfully gone outside. Ellie invited him only because her father insisted (she didn't say, but Ilya knew), thinking he wouldn't say yes.

Standing in front of the hollow house, he closed his eyes. The swim of red and gold behind his lids.

He hid in the room above his sister's boathouse. He didn't trust cities anymore.

As he walked to the lawyer's office from the subway, the billows of plastic sheeting shrouding the skyscrapers under construction were like sails, and the obelisks underneath could drift toward him. Crushed. No one would notice. He couldn't pay attention when the lawyer spoke. Didn't the man understand he was about to disappear?

He swayed on the edge of the curb. He should not smoke before eating, his mother would tell him if he was answering her calls, her paranoid texts. He'd answer soon. His mother, his father. They made him so tired.

Across the street, the curtains twitched.

The lawyer was a crook the wives had found on the side of a suburban bus, gleaming teeth and gelled ridges of hair. In the office, Ilya pushed his chair back, pulled his cap low over his eyes. The two widows didn't look at him. They hated him for being alive.

He hadn't really known their husbands, thickset bullish men who were friends, their scorn hiding how not at home they were in this outer edge of the city, which probably looked almost identical to the outer edge of the city they'd emigrated from: concrete high-rises, rows of failing storefronts. But not home, or not yet. They spoke only Russian to one another, and Ilya, his accent painstakingly outgrown, pretended not to understand. He listened, hoping to take offence at an insult to himself, but there was none. They thought nothing about him.

He was still dizzy. Not again, not the panic, it was just the cigarette, he felt the curb falling away and sat without meaning to, stretching his legs into the street.

The lawyer's office smelled like that pine air freshener his mother loved. It made Ilya's eyes water. He pulled the brim of his cap lower, and the women looked away. One was very young, younger than Ilya. Ilya recognized her pinched profile, though in the pictures the dead man had shown Ilya, thick makeup rendered her face smoothly pink. She was not made up now, like this was a way to show she was mourning. Her skin was blotchy, a red patch on her left cheek like she'd been slapped. Her accent was heavier than her husband's. She was a receptionist in a dentist's office; one photograph showed her in pale blue, sitting in a swivel chair under blanching fluorescents. The young wife's smile was identical in every picture, Ilya saw with contempt as he thumbed across the screen, her head held at the same angle. She must have practised her face in front of the mirror. Pert, hint of a sneer.

That face was gone. She had no face left. She must have really loved that stump-fingered man easily ten years older than her. Ilya pulled at the brim of his hat. The other widow grilled the lawyer, took notes in a spiral notebook with a cluster of roses on the cover.

Ilya waited for the women to accuse him. Someone must be responsible. That was what the lawyer said. There was no such thing as bad luck, the wind twisting at the right moment, the undetectable fault in the scaffold. Someone must be responsible, why not Ilya? He was more experienced, working for the company for six years, valuable as the men were not, fluent in English, a citizen. He could have inspected the harness, shouted a warning in the teeth of the wind, grasped the rope as the husbands clutched his boots in a heroic finale, swinging together as the platform fell, pulled back inside just as Ilya couldn't hold on anymore.

The curtain shifted. The old woman watched him. Baba Yaga gnawing men's bones in her chicken-leg hut. She saw his weakness.

He stood up. Behind him, the sound of water rose from the hole. Then the pump again. The river running underneath.

Ellie lived by a river. She'd set her sights on a different life: studying nutrition and marrying young, a shy accountant who, Ilya thought, would not dream of leaving her and whose air of baffled resignation complemented her strategizing. She'd probably made him fill out a compatibility chart on their second date. Together they moved to outside a small town where they knew no one, raised petulant children Ilya rarely saw. Ellie worked, alongside a massage therapist, a chiropractor, and two beauticians who offered facials and handmade creams, in a pretty building that called itself a wellness clinic. She collected mottos engraved on stones, placed them in her garden, which she told Ilya he should work in once his hands healed. Gardening was therapeutic. He didn't want to work in her stupid garden. The flowers smelled like the bath bombs she kept in a bowl on the back of the toilet. He stood on the path she'd gravelled and read her mottos:

Believe
Dare to Dream
Pray
Friendship Is Forever
No Mistakes Only Opportunities
Family Is Everything

From a safe distance, his niece and nephew watched him.

In the boathouse, he slept late, the sky changing as he lay in bed. He loved the circular skylight, the blue disc growing gold in the afternoon, leaching into violet, then grey and then black, but the sky was never black, he'd thought outside the city it would be black. It was the deepest blue. Lying in bed, he drank water and ate chips, licking the salt off his fingertips. His bandages were off. The leaves were falling. He thought of himself on the camping trip as a boy, lying in the tent watching the branches outlined by the moonlight above his head. How the world looked like fractals, how he was part of it, how he'd thought he would be spared disaster. The sound of the cars from the nearby highway reminded him of waves. The tent was floating on the ocean.

Ellie didn't ask him anything. She was eight years older, the daughter of his mother's husband. His stepfather insisted they were siblings, as if they could share a history that didn't exist. They'd only lived together three years in that apartment; Ellie was dutiful, helping his mother with dinner, picking him up from the aftercare program at school. Sometimes he'd catch her looking at him when her father tried out his clumsy patriarchal heartiness, demonstrating that he, unlike Ilya's banished father, was a responsible man who should be better appreciated. Ilya had appreciated him, up to a point. Not the point of telling him. And then he'd died. Too late now.

Ilya guessed Ellie pitied the small quiet boy he'd been, but distantly, because she had to make her own plans for escape. All the time she must have held this happy ending in her head: the bungalow, the path down to the swift river, the boathouse with the motorboat and two canoes, the bathroom and bedroom above it decorated in blue and yellow. She called it a guesthouse, but he didn't know for what guests, she seemed to have very few friends, in spite of her mottoes. He dozed for days under the blindingly white duvet, looking at his phone, examining his sleeve tattoos, his muscles growing slack. How loose his arms would be when he was old, he could see it waiting for him, the slouch of his aged skin. The falling men had opened a wide swinging space under his feet. The wide space was inside him now.

He shrugged when Ellie asked him how long he would stay. Where would he go?

Ellie's husband, the accountant, seemed startled by the noisy demands of his children (they were always demanding new phones or bikes or trips, different clothes, different food). The husband was necessary and irrelevant, and Ilya despised him. Ellie needed him for his capacity to make money, enabling the sculpted paths and the bedroom over the boathouse and the cast-iron fire bowl circled with logs that no one sat at because they were indoors in front of the television. And she needed him as a vision of a husband: his fond silence, his willingness to bow to her judgments. She'd imagined him along with everything else, as she sat studying at the fake mahogany table that was far too big for their cramped apartment. Ilya admired Ellie's will, making a life she'd had no birthright to, extracted from magazines, from websites. And sometimes, when Ilya made himself join the family at dinner, there'd be a moment of the setting sun catching the square green plates and heavy forks, the water pitcher and the single bottle of white wine and the salad full of nuts and berries (he remembered childhood's lumps of iceberg lettuce in Kraft dressing), and the children would stop bickering and appear as remote and beautiful as Ellie did, taking her husband's hand across the table, satisfied with her efforts, as if she at last inhabited one of those design websites she'd studied, thinking, *That is what I want.*

The curb was still falling. The old woman watched. Baba Yaga in his mother's stories, the witch in the wood, you must approach her respectfully, in the right way, or she will eat you.

When he threw his shaved-off hair into the trees, he didn't leave the path, thinking of woods, frightened of the dusk. The hair fell anticlimactically, drifting in the branches of a stand of red-berried bushes. He went back to the boathouse and looked at his phone again.

Cover-ups, backroom deals, the hale faces of men in expensive suits, the head of Navigator and the police (cops, fucking cops), some of it sounded crazy, but Ilya knew enough about history to know that not every crackpot is wrong, and who cares, he thought, scrolling and clicking, lying back and letting the stories wash over him, who cares and who's to say what's real, he didn't believe in anything, he could believe in everything, why not, giant lizards and deep states and the masterminding of 9/11 by American politicians to justify oil wars (*We need a Pearl Harbor,* Rumsfeld said, he *said* it, people heard him), aborted fetuses in vaccines, the moon landing was faked (look at the flag), JFK (beautiful Jackie in the bloodstained dress), the Illuminati (he loved old maps and charts, he wanted secrets to be fearsome and elegant), men with hunting rifles crashing through the B.C. Interior looking for Bigfoot, chemtrails (as a boy he'd lain on his back in the grass admiring the plumes of white). Why not believe in all of it? Believe in wild lawlessness, in Trump extracting Ukraine's rare earth metals so Elon Musk could ride a spaceship to Mars? Ilya didn't know if that was even that bad an idea. Maybe there were no bad ideas. Ilya didn't mind. Ilya could believe everything and find it beautiful. Let the metals come out of the bloody earth. Let the red planet teem with unlikely life. Let everything burn.

But when he put his phone away, he became again a person who believed in nothing and envied people who believed.

The men screamed as they fell.

He'd shut his eyes. Before they hit the ground. He'd shut his eyes.

Someone must be held responsible.

His hands healed, hardened. The raised scars were still there, embedded underneath his regrown skin.

His cigarette was almost finished. From the men on the porch, that same song again, 'Gimme Shelter.' Why did they keep playing it? Did they think there was a mystery they could uncover? They seemed stupid like that, nodding their heads at hidden meaning. There wasn't any. Why did they think there was meaning? He hated that song. Rape, murder. You don't pretend those things. He wanted to shout at them that you don't *pretend* those things.

The older men dressed in workboots but weren't working, the younger man with the long pink scar on his face, Ilya thought it might be from a burn, the man with the dragging leg whose mother was Baba Yaga and gnawed leg bones, the fat woman with the dog, they were all there, listening, laughing, listening again, thinking there was meaning., Ilya hated them and envied them.

Across the street the curtains moved. Baba Yaga in her dangerous house.

He tasted the filter, threw the cigarette into the street, and turned away before it hit the pavement.

On the porch, the men laughed around her, but she ignored them, lit a cigarette. She would get up in a minute and buy that rope at the hardware store. She was handed another beer, already cracked for her, she liked the signal, the tiny fizzing in her head.

The blue velour was damp under her arms. When she was younger, she hated sweat stains on her clothes, the antiperspirant made her skin tighten and itch, now she didn't give a shit. Let them notice the darkening circles at her armpits, she ran her hand through her hair, shaking the length over one shoulder and admiring the flash of the dye. She leaned back and blew smoke rings, and when she opened her eyes, that skinny scared woman was watching her from across the street. She was carrying a bag, she'd been crying, what the fuck did she have to cry about? Maybe her husband was a pervert, you never knew by looking, the stories she'd heard, she nodded to herself, you never knew. What was that story her grandmother used to tell her, the woman keeps asking for more and more from this magic fish her husband catches until she asks to be God and then she's back in the shack? Her grandmother got very serious in the part about wanting to be God, she was so Catholic, but that wasn't the point, the point was that the crying woman didn't know she'd find herself back in the shack one of these days. Fucking men.

Why was the woman still looking at her? She took another drag, winked, but the woman didn't seem to notice she was trying to stare her down, the woman thought everyone loved her.

Then something happened, the woman was really looking at her, like the woman saw her younger, when she'd swaggered in and out of the pool halls along Dundas, her hair in a ponytail, her hands on her studded belt, so late it was morning. Like the woman was remembering her then, which was bullshit, she'd have been a kid, she could see her as a kid, in a white dress on a tire swing in a big yard, the red hair hanging down, not a mark anywhere, she knew nothing, so how was it the woman was standing with her weight on one hip, like she was under a street light just before dawn?

She settled deeper into the folding chair, thinking of herself in her acid-wash jeans and tank top and her hair in the tight high ponytail. She didn't dye it then (did that woman dye her hair?), it swung and brushed at her neck, and she smashed her beer bottles into the curb, dark glass exploding around her boots. Moving from place to place like a shark, that was what sharks did, just kept moving until they died, she'd step out of the way of the flying glass and ignore whatever was shouted after her.

The woman should wear sunglasses so it wasn't so obvious she'd cried, she had no self-respect, showing herself like that. Idiot. When she was young, younger than the woman, she'd known not to let anyone know she wanted anything, asking for anything will keep you from being a shark swimming, from tossing your beer bottle at the curb and walking away, dangerous as a knife in a boot, she'd never carried a knife but she looked like she did and that did the trick. The woman starting walking again, turned at the corner down her street. Good for you, baby girl. Move along. Figure out how to be a shark before it's too late.

She should go. Her dog was waiting on the porch, chewing on his rope like he had a plan. But she was so tired suddenly, thinking of herself and all these streets and that sad dumb woman who didn't know you couldn't show you were disappointed, like you were owed everything, like someone was going to waltz in and tell you it was okay, don't worry, honey, you can be God.

If she stood in that one spot behind her curtains, she could watch the young man working without being seen from the street.

The woman across the street had left her child alone. The little boy with his cape. She'd left him watching television. That used to be okay, but it wasn't now.

She never answered Bobby's texts, but she carried the phone in the pocket of her housedress, the texts blinking orange on the dark screen, just in case. She watched the boy sitting on the couch and wondered if she could call someone, she disliked speaking English and the small hard buttons hurt her fingers, but she liked the idea that she could report something. Bobby would know who she should call. He liked to know what was best. As a child he told her she was wrong about everything, his father knew more, his teacher, his friends, the parents of his friends, anyone but her. Now he wanted her to move into an apartment. He knew what she should want. Years ago, decades ago, she'd told her sons (not in anger but in surprise, didn't they understand?) that what they wanted didn't matter. They couldn't expect it to matter, who did they think they were?

She didn't know who she thought she was, that she wanted what she wanted to matter now. Bobby didn't care, and Gabriel didn't make decisions, he was not able to make decisions. He would never leave her. He had never tried to.

Who did she think she was? She must be no one. Standing behind her curtains watching the young man smoke and the little boy watch television, she felt the light begin to shine through her. She wouldn't call anyone. The buttons hurt her fingers. Bobby paid for the phone, brought it on one of his visits from North York, he came every two weeks and yelled at Gabriel for his uselessness, he showed her how to use the phone. Her fingers were soft now (she'd been proud of her calluses).

It was a flip phone. Gabriel said Bobby was cheap, but he said it after Bobby left, when they were eating dinner (she peeled the covers off the trays and slid them into the microwave, if her mother could see her). Bobby was with his family, he never stayed to eat. Gabriel would not say anything to Bobby's face, Bobby would have a smiling angry reply, jeering at his older brother, who had to beg her for cigarette money. She'd ask him to bring her purse.

Bobby called him Gabe. He wanted everyone to call him Gabe. His name was Gabriel, angel of the annunciation. When he was dead, God would call him Gabriel. When he was a kid, he'd said, *Gabe Ma please Gabe please.* She would not. God would call him Gabriel, and when he was dead he would become who he was meant to be (she didn't know who; God did).

She thought maybe it was one of Emily's old phones that Bobby gave her, not even something he'd bought specially. Emily came once a month with her mother, she hated how polite Emily was, the accidental baby with his second wife (Bobby's other children were grown and elsewhere, she had great-grandchildren, she couldn't remember their names). When she spoke to Emily, Emily looked up from her screen, smiled, looked down again, keeping the smile. Emily looked like her mother. That same surprised smile, like they weren't sure why you were talking to them. But Bobby was happy, she knew that, she couldn't help seeing how he watched his wife, how pleased and helpless he seemed, like he couldn't believe his luck. If she'd still gone to church, she'd have confessed to the priest. How it made her jealous because no one had ever looked at her like that, never in her life. It was unfair. Sometimes she thought she hadn't known that look existed. It was so far from anything she'd been allowed to expect for herself. And she'd been shocked when Bobby married again, quickly enough it was obvious why he'd finally asked for a divorce after decades of grudging truce.

Who did he think he was, to demand happiness? To act like he had a right to it?

Gabriel didn't have a phone. He had no money. Anyway, he didn't need one, he never left the neighbourhood, he walked the same loops, the same streets, the streets of his childhood and his whole life, there was grey in his hair, she was so old.

The child was still watching television.

She had the phone in her pocket. When she shifted, she felt it bounce against her hip.

The young man lit another cigarette. He was sitting on the curb. Something was wrong with him. She could see something was wrong. He didn't know he was beautiful, in the way that anyone young is beautiful (she'd cried in front of the mirror, examining her young body, she'd had no idea, what a waste). He moved like a snapped power line.

There was the woman coming home with her shopping bag. So she wouldn't be able to call anyone. The young man stood up. He liked watching the little boy's mother, and she liked watching him, and they both pretended. Sometimes the woman complained about the rats. She was afraid of them and told him it was his fault, but the whole street was full of rats. If the woman would listen to her (but she didn't leave her house anymore and no one wanted to listen), she would have told her not to think about the rats. There had always been rats. These streets were their homes. When she was younger than the woman (but she'd never had such hair, she would have loved hair like that), she'd known the only thing was a truce. Keep the kitchen clean, keep the yard clean (she'd washed the front steps with bleach, on her knees), and the rats would stay in their own places, the tunnels under the fence, the basement. Her basement was criss-crossed with the paths of rats, they could chew through anything, you couldn't keep them out. She was not afraid if they kept to their own places. Though when she'd gone down into her basement, she'd felt the rats watching her, those were the only stairs she was afraid of then, picking her way down in the glare of the naked bulb, seeing herself falling, twisted on the concrete floor, and the rats sniffing, curious, then hungry. A whisper, a rustle behind the old suitcases and the cardboard boxes of Bobby's sports trophies. Gone when she looked.

The man and the woman were still on the pavement. The child was still watching TV. She turned away from the window, walked slowly to the stairs. The stairs were one of Bobby's arguments, he wanted her to sleep in the living room, he would put in a bathroom off the kitchen, or they would sell the house, she could move into one of those retirement apartments he'd made her go see. She would not. What would happen to Gabriel? Gabriel needed her so she could keep her house, she wouldn't have to go inside that box, the apartments were very clean, but in her dreams they were coffins.

Going upstairs was hardest. She tried not to hurry, though she could feel the possibility of an accident. That sudden terrible warmth like blood. She crept on all fours so at least if she slipped she'd slide on her front, not backward. Almost there, she could see the open bathroom door to the right of the stairs. She straightened up, reached for the banister, and fell, clutching the air, all the way down.

Milo liked being alone in the house. And one of the episodes had made him think of a plan. It wasn't formed yet, just a hunch of something he wanted. The arc of metal flung through open space on the screen, the crash of something falling hard into darkness. Maybe, if he timed it right for later in the day, he could do it. He liked to think about what might happen. If anything would happen. He wanted to make something happen. He was a winner. Winners made things happen. Outside, the smoke drifted through the screen. The smell was leafy, warm. This was what it felt like to be an adult. No one could ask you how you felt or where you were going. He hummed a song, not the song from the show, a song he was practising in his room, or in the bathroom, where he could see his face in the mirror, holding his head like the singer, chin tilted right and lifted. Narrowed eyes. He could see the audience watching him. But an audience only watches, they are not allowed to ask. You give what you like, but no one asks. He looked up. His mother was at the window.

'I didn't know I'd be gone that long.'

Ilya was startled; he didn't think she'd speak. 'What?'

'I had to get something from the store. I thought I'd be quicker.'

She was smiling, thinking he'd noticed she was gone. Well, he had, he'd seen the boy behind the curtain, so she was right. He didn't know if he liked her guessing that he thought of her. She was smiling, but he could see she'd cried. Grey stains under her eyes, how soft the skin looked there, horribly soft, like he was seeing something too private, the very slight hollowing in the skin under her eyes, velvety, thinned. He was seized with embarrassment, like panic, the curb falling away again, this feeling she expected something, that he ought to have something to say to her, something important she had a right to expect, she was standing in front of him like she had rights to him. She saw it, the wide space inside him, that was why she didn't mind showing him she'd been crying, because she could see the space inside him, soon he wouldn't be able to hide it anymore, not from anyone, he must do something drastic to hide it, he must say something, he could think of nothing, she was waiting on him, wearing the courteous expectant smile women gave, assuming he would know what they meant. Women like her, he thought, but he didn't think she was a woman like that: he didn't know enough about her. If there hadn't been a space inside him with the wind pushing through it, he might have known what to say, but the wind was loud, like the sound of a piece of metal scraping across the floor of an abandoned house. The cigarette butts lay at his feet, and he couldn't tell if she noticed. He retreated before she could ask him for anything. Waited on the other side of the door, how long she seemed to stand there (in his panic he thought he could feel her breathing) before he heard the sigh of her door, the greeting she called to her son (she wouldn't show her boy she'd cried, she would only show Ilya), the bolt springing back into place. Like she'd hoped he'd come back outside.

In the playground, they found a broken beer bottle someone had thrown against the low wall separating the school's property from the sidewalk. Brown glass, warm from the sun, the dried beer smeared along the curves like a gasoline slick on the surface of water. Sylvie saw the glass first, just as Clio was about to suggest they leave, and Sylvie was afraid Clio would go home and tell her she didn't want to see her until Nat took them to the café. Sylvie knew what the glass would mean, and Clio would be impressed that she'd pointed it out. The last time she'd said no.

Sylvie picked up a square shard, and Clio, allowing the importance of the moment, held out her hand. She would go first, as was right, which would make it impossible for Sylvie to change her mind, Sylvie knew she couldn't recover from another refusal. Clio thrust her pointer finger at the shard Sylvie held, and Sylvie closed her eyes, kept her hand steady. When she opened her eyes, she saw a red bead on the tip of Clio's finger, like the stones in one of her mother's necklaces. It was her turn.

'Don't worry,' Clio said tenderly, 'it doesn't hurt, it's nothing.' Sylvie remembered how quiet Clio could be, how gentle, even when she was speaking to the girl at school who they hated. Especially then. Sylvie held out her hand, made herself steady, and it was worth it if Clio wanted her again; she thrust her hand at Clio hard and Clio didn't move fast enough or didn't move on purpose and the shard missed her finger and sliced a red line along Sylvie's palm, surprising how clear and precise the pain was, and yet foreign, as if it was happening to someone else.

Clio pulled back the glass, waited to see what Sylvie would do. Sylvie wanted to scream and run, she could feel herself moving home, shrieking so people burst through their screen doors as she passed, but instead she looked at her hand, the fine blade of a scythe running along it, and licked the blood into a pink smear. Clio's eyes widened, she had amazed Clio, she had not forgotten how.

'You're right. It doesn't hurt at all.'

Nat considered whether she needed to buy groceries and thought of the dead woman who had lived in her house. Her ghost was a hunch Nat paid attention to occasionally when she was alone. The old woman had been banished: the ripped-out first floor, the new kitchen with the hard light pouring from the sliding glass doors. And yet. Younger, working on the PhD she never finished, she'd read ghost stories voraciously, sitting up late at night, the drip from the tap or the snicker of a door hinge signs of presences she couldn't see.

She was not alone; she could hear Felix shuffling upstairs.

What was he doing? What was he thinking?

Resisting calling him, she turned on the CBC, but it was the end-of-the-world sound. A musician friend who'd become a producer on one of those irksome pop-culture shows had told Nat she'd know something was really wrong when the station played bad jazz from 1963. The friend meant technical difficulties, but since then Nat heard calamity in the banal notes.

It would happen slowly, then quickly.

She'd turn on the faucet and there'd be a yellowish tinge to the water.

Lights flickering.

The grid blinking off. People trying to stumble home. Thinking it was fun at first, like the blackout in 2003. Until everyone realized this was not an aberration, it was a beginning.

Then something big, a plane falling from the sky, an apocalyptic roar of metal cratering a neighbourhood, people in kitchens, new kitchens like hers, snatched efficiently from their lives.

Tanks rolling in.

Governments descending to whatever bomb shelters were prepared for them.

The super-rich sealing themselves in their secret chambers.

The jazz was the sound of ruin. Ruin was everywhere.

She switched it off.

Sometimes her annoyance at the CBC propelled her in her tasks (did she need more tomato paste?), like the jittery pleasure of too much coffee. She sternly lectured an imaginary listener, or Frankie when Frankie was home, on shallow progressivism masking nationalist sentimentalities. Frankie, exasperated, told her to stop listening, Frankie would not concern herself with the apocalypse or Felix upstairs.

She typed *are we okay*. She added a question mark, put down her phone, picked it up again, erased the message without sending it. Typed *I'm sorry* and erased it.

She heard Felix go into the bathroom. She should make him lunch. Clio had asked for her allowance, she and Sylvie would eat those greasy squares of cardboard from the pizza place on the corner where Nat suspected Clio bullied Sylvie into buying pop for her, which she wasn't allowed. Her allowance was smaller than Sylvie's. Nat wanted Clio to understand that money meant something. Frankie was less sure this was wise, if a smaller allowance just convinced Clio she was owed Sylvie's, to balance the injustice of being born to parents with a weakness for ideological points. Frankie earned handsomely, something she enjoyed saying in quotations, as if she was the paterfamilias of a Victorian household, relishing how thoroughly they'd left their old selves behind. Going from deluded PhD students in a basement apartment who bought clothes from the Goodwill and allowed themselves a pitcher of cheap beer here and there to inhabitants of this pristinely gutted and reconfigured house, secure while the city around them grew more and more attenuated, full of people who didn't have the time to meditate on final disaster, they were too preoccupied with the smaller disaster of their daily lives, spent trying to stay one step ahead of money, failing, falling.

Felix came downstairs, dressed.

'Where are you going, sweetie?'

'Out.'

She heard the front door close. He never slammed doors.

Nat wanted to run after him and tell him to avoid the walking man. She should have said something to Clio earlier too, Clio was interested in provocation, and the girls might antagonize the man the way they would poke at a wounded wasp with a stick. Nat knew this was more Clio than Sylvie, but Clio was her problem. Yet she had friends, she was tough as a diamond, she thrived; Nat didn't want to also think of Clio as a problem. She didn't have the time to spare for the problem of Clio.

Maddy thought Clio was a problem. Last week she'd asked Nat to go out for lunch. Nat arrived already wary; they never saw each other without children, when they talked all afternoon it was impromptu, one inviting the other inside on a whim, letting the afternoon run down without meaning to. Nat didn't think of Maddy as a close friend; she had her other friends, known for decades, with whom she had a store of shared opinions, shared jokes. On the phone to these old friends, she called Maddy *the actress* and told amusing stories about her, made her a stand-in for all self-absorbed straight women who treated their husbands with a mixture of deference and contempt, and if the actual details of Nat's days closely resembled Maddy's, the old friends didn't point it out.

The restaurant was very bright. Nat felt herself under observation, touching the display case with one hand, her fingers leaving a smudge that made the young server wince. She expanded under his gaze, frumpily queer and middle-aged, her scarf half falling off her neck, her coat bulky, retrieved from the closet when the day was unexpectedly cold. Sitting across from Maddy, she'd been conscious of the crumbs from her sandwich clinging to the front of her shirt, a small grease stain she'd just noticed over her left breast. Blunted by this, she didn't realize the import of the conversation (overthinking, Frankie said, listening faithfully later).

Maddy sat very straight and ate her pasta salad one noodle at a time, circling back to the girls, which made sense, there'd been that meeting at school about the classmate; Sylvie and Clio had left some mean drawings in her desk. When they got up to leave, Nat understood. *She thinks everything is Clio's fault.* Maddy had to go to the gym (she never missed a day), and Nat walked home thinking cruel things she could have said about Milo or about Maddy's marriage. Nat didn't like Alex very much but she believed she liked him better than Maddy did. Maddy was loyal in how she spoke of him, more loyal than Nat, who'd been letting herself slip, complaining about Frankie's obliviousness, her absence. It was dangerous. She knew it was dangerous. Though Frankie didn't seem to find Nat's complaining dangerous, she took it in stride, poured overlarge scotches and laughed at her, Frankie couldn't be destroyed as Alex would be when Maddy finally let loose. Nat wondered what would happen to Alex when Maddy blew up his life. He had no idea.

She typed *I'm sorry about this morning* and erased it.

Felix is more unhappy than is normal she typed, and erased it.

The old woman in Nat's house had died at eighty-four, sitting down in her kitchen to light a cigarette after wheeling her cart home from the grocery store. When the ambulance came, the old woman was already dead, slumped in the chair, the fallen cigarette burning a hole in the linoleum.

The hole was gone, the floor was gone. But the longer they lived in the house (it was twelve years now, almost), the more Nat thought about the old woman. They'd moved into it in a fog, small baby, sudden chance, the real estate agent chirping, *So much work just to make it livable,* and Nat knew what she meant, but someone had lived here, for decades, making do with the badly fitting windows, the slow leaks in the bathroom, and the ineptly painted kitchen, the walls so stained with smoke that the removed pictures were still visible in outline, like the shape of a cross on the living room wall.

Frankie watched Nat despair over the plight of the old woman as they discovered more damp patches under the sink, rags stuffed in the cracks, and asked if it was like Nat's grandmother's house. Nat, trying to scrape up loosened strips of wallpaper, shook her head impatiently without turning. Felix, who Frankie was nursing on the sofa they'd pushed to the middle of the room, fussed and belched and slept. Frankie, her childhood spent in the suburbs of a smaller city, seemed to picture sordid chaos when Nat talked about her grandmother's house, the rows of canned food, the disaster supplies in the basement.

To be fair, Nat imagined Frankie, embryonically butch, with braces and skinned knees, biking along sunny cul-de-sacs, as if her childhood were a commercial for an insurance company. When they'd met, Nat was only just training herself to stop smiling with her mouth closed to hide her crooked teeth; the other graduate students all seemed to come from households where braces were afforded, and Nat had decided her teeth were a badge of honour, proving she'd worked harder than they had. But that didn't mean her grandmother lived in chaos. And yet (Nat thought, composing and erasing texts) something in the house before they made it theirs did remind her of her grandmother's house. The rage and loneliness of old women nobody wants.

Where was Felix going?

The walking man had left the porch, it was just the three usual men and the glaring woman with the dog. Her grandmother, ferociously tidy, spraying pesticide on her pink roses, would have despised them.

Where was Felix?

Nat took comfort in developmental theories about twelve-year-old boys, hoarded descriptions of locked doors and long silences. Until she was caught off guard by Felix's sadness, how ill at ease he was in his body. She read too much online, her work didn't occupy enough of her mind. She wrote grants for art galleries and small literary organizations, the most useful thing available for a person with an unfinished PhD in Victorian poetry and less ambition than she'd planned on. It suited the family when the kids were small and Frankie had just started her new job, but now Felix's unhappiness filled Nat's days. They were the same, she thought, hitting out at the kindness that surrounded them, his body suddenly unfamiliar to him, as hers was. She couldn't tell him that; he would have been mortified.

She didn't need groceries. She put away her phone. Frankie could text first. Ten minutes with the novel she was reading about the young woman who went to live in an almost empty room in a foreign city.

The novel's few characters appeared to live without plastic or the internet, which to Nat seemed like dire rivers she swam in, on the verge of panic, a manageable panic like a manageable pain. Refreshing her phone to skim across the surface of disasters understood to be harbingers of a cataclysm so total it would mean the end of everything (the tap dripped yellow, the lights flickered, the plane fell to earth). The things she read about were heralds: invasions, wildfires, the rise of the new right, the problem of the puritanical left. She felt the ridges of her brain grow smooth through steady low-level assault the way a stone grows smooth over centuries on a beach.

The young protagonist, thinking on love and art, floated above these rivers. Perhaps plastic was a quibble, Nat thought, flipping to the back of the book. But plastic seemed central, infusing everyone's life, her life (she looked at her kitchen shelves, at the ingredients laid on the table, spice jars, the bottle of Worcestershire sauce on the counter), packaged food catching the light through the new glass doors. Novels needed to have plastic in them, it was everywhere, the print of red roses and green leaves on the pasta, the rabbit on the organic crackers. Ripped apart, crunched into the trash. When she looked at her kitchen, she saw the garbage streaming out of it like that was what happened after you died, you were shown your own garbage, slippery white grocery bags fluttering in the cold wind of the afterworld like handkerchiefs waving from the deck of a departing ship in a black-and-white photograph.

The author photo showed a beautiful young woman on a balcony. Nat pictured her alone in a large European city, the balcony overlooking a quiet street. She closed the book and pushed it across the table, watched it fall off the edge, let it lie on the floor.

Her own house was so silent. When Milo wiped his mouth on Maddy's shirt, Nat felt relief that she'd passed that time. Felix twelve, Clio ten. They'd had them close together, trying to move swiftly through the murk of diapers, mashed food, tears, especially since they were both nearing forty when Felix was born, they had been unsure for a long time, debating who should carry the children, Nat didn't want to, she was afraid it would obliterate her, and then it had taken a long time for success.

Marshalling her ingredients, she minced the onions, slid the sprouting hearts from the garlic with the point of her knife, lifted the pork shoulder out of the butcher paper, leaving a watery red trail from the counter to the frying pan. Fumbling with two wooden spoons, she turned the meat, the haunch hissing as it browned. Pulled pork was inelegant, but the children would eat it, and she would make her own buns and a salad of dark greens. The house would smell like meat.

She wanted the dinner to be a success. Frankie would come home penitently and tell her she was right, they would pay better attention to Felix, and Frankie would fold napkins, the guests would wipe grease from their fingers and the corners of their mouths. Frankie would tease her, compliment her, drink more than her, together they would keep the evening going, their marriage obviously the stronger, there'd be a theatricality to this, the way

Frankie allowed herself to be cast as Alex's ersatz counterpart, and Alex, flattered, would accept a second beer. She and Frankie would show each other off, Frankie smiling at her over Alex's shoulder, and Felix would be withdrawn, not enough to distress the guests, just enough to prove Nat right, she wanted to be right, she didn't try to help it, alone in her kitchen she wanted to imagine a look on Frankie's face, watching Felix, seeing how much she had missed, a stricken look only Nat would catch. Frankie would recover herself, Alex would blunder on, Maddy nervously braiding and unbraiding her hair. The four of them would complain about the construction on the house, the men on the porch, the threat of the walking man. The girls would speak only to each other, Felix to no one, Milo would sing Disney songs at the table, immune to any sense of his own imposition, belting the high note of one of those manifest-destiny songs that Nat remembered reliably came in around the twenty-minute mark as the heroine gazed at the horizon and knew there must be more. More what? More. Just more.

But she didn't want to be right about Felix. She wanted him to catch her eye in the middle of Milo singing, like he used to, she wanted them to share the joke of Milo across the table. Felix didn't want to share jokes anymore.

And Alex would ask rhetorically if the walking man seemed angrier, more volatile. Nat wouldn't disagree with Alex, but he thought something should be done and she couldn't see what. She told her children to cross the street when they saw him. Anyone would.

She lifted the pork out of the pan and into the slow cooker, simmered the fat with spices and tomatoes, onions and garlic, cursed as the pan almost slipped from her hands, made inept by the oven mitts.

The house smelled like meat. It was the smell of her grandmother's house, though there mixed with bleach, where they went once a week for the awful dinner. Nat ordered to help while her younger brother sprawled on the couch, Nat's mother twitchy in the kitchen doorway drinking wine, not helping, keeping up her litany of complaints: the stupid cows in the office, her shitty boss, and this, Nat understood even at twelve, was meant to subdue Nat's grandmother, put her in her place as Nat put her own mother in her place with bespoke butcher shops and cloth napkins.

What did Felix understand? Maybe that was the terror of children: they watched you without giving away what they understood.

Nat and Nick (Natasha and Nicholas, her mother must have wanted porcelain dolls, not children) lived with their mother in an area now resplendently unrecognizable with coffee shops and boutiques, but when Nat was twelve it seemed so far from everywhere. The city had been different, she insisted to her children when trying to make them understand their lives as opulent to the point of absurdity. She painted her childhood as more careworn than was strictly true. She and Nick let themselves in after school until it was time to heat up dinner, but they had a house, small and chosen for cheapness (her mother's job was clerical, her professional intrigues exaggerated), though just as much for being on the opposite end of the city from Nat's grandmother, who assumed they would move in with her when Nat's father left.

'Fuck that, I'm not living with those plastic flowers,' Nat's mother said. Not the plastic flowers or plastic-covered furniture or her grandmother's air of grudging concession, as if she knew better than her daughter, better than anyone, but would not insist. She knew she would be proved right in time. Fires burning all around her, she would sit on her pile of cans and dispense secret wisdom. She should have become a Jehovah's Witness or joined a cult, Nat thought, it would have given her some company. But there was more dignity in being alone. Stockpiling supplies in the basement because the bad times were coming back, and she would be ready.

Nat's mother had no dignity, flummoxing the friends Nat (still Natasha then) wanted, friends who lived in larger, messier houses, who went to cottages and summer camps and music lessons (Nat's only extra lesson was Russian heritage language). Nat's mother gave offence easily and was easily offended. She called people idiots to their faces, jabbed the air with her fork as she ate. Nat/Natasha stopped asking classmates home, seeing their confusion at her mother's invective, at her accent. She went to their houses when asked, not often enough.

By twelve she'd decided her mother plotted to make her unhappy, not yet understanding that her mother didn't often think of Nat, lost in her own trajectory, hitting out haplessly at receding targets. Her mother, gaunt (Nat was not), stopped suddenly in mid-tirade, her thinning dry hair electric in the forced air from the vents in Nat's grandmother's tiny kitchen, and told Nat she would get her new clothes, she was too old for what she was wearing. *Good girl,* said her grandmother, and Nat crossed her arms over her chest, her new breasts itching like scabs.

When they finished eating, they couldn't leave, her mother needed to prolong her own irritation, and they sat on the couch watching TV. Her mother and grandmother painted their nails, cotton balls nudged between their toes, the gleaming small brushes pinched expertly between finger and thumb.

'Come here. Let's do your nails. Don't you want to be pretty?'

She shook her head, so angry she felt her face grow hot.

'Look! Mama, she's blushing. So shy.'

'She wants to be pretty.'

Thankfully, Nat's mother shrugged, losing interest. 'Leave her alone. Anyway, she has her father's feet.'

They looked down at Nat's toes, went back to their task. Nat, crouched in the armchair, examined her despised father's feet, broad and flat, the nails brittle. She would never have their narrow feet or their skill, and the bloody shine of their toenails was an innate knowledge she could not absorb. She couldn't transcend her feet or the stubborn lumps of her breasts; she couldn't change anything about herself, and her efforts would fail.

Looking up from her feet, she studied the picture on her grandmother's wall. A framed print she'd bought at a garage sale, showing a dirt road lined with trees. The trees turning black, the road grey as the sun set. The painting, in her memory (she picked up the book from the kitchen floor, smoothing the pages), was conventionally photographic, probably mid-nineteenth century, each branch defined, each leaf. It was the light that held her eyes, the way the painter had conveyed the thin gold of evening emptying into white.

Nat picked up the frying pan, it was cool enough for that. That light was difficult, it needed restraint, emptiness, a huge emptiness that other abstractions only hinted at. The light draining out was the ordinary end of the day and the end of the world as well. That was why she wanted to look at it.

She liked the fading warmth of the cast iron.

She saw her brother only a few times a year, though they lived in the same city. Frankie was close to her older brothers (who had been suspicious of Nat for years, almost fatherly in their conviction that she was so lucky to have Frankie, did she appreciate it? Which was probably a fair question).

Turning up the heat on the slow cooker, she thought Felix and Clio would not want to see each other once they'd escaped their upbringing. They would have nothing to say. She washed the cast iron without soap, laid it on the blue flame, hung it on the hook beside the spice rack.

She'd always thought of her mother as the Fisherman's Wife. The fisherman catches a magic flounder and the flounder grants him a wish in exchange for freedom, and so the man asks for a little house instead of his leaking hut. His wife makes him go back again and again, each time with a new wish. She wants servants, she wants a palace, she wants to be the emperor, she wants to be God. And that is the last straw, the flounder sends them back to their hut and is never seen again. Her mother with all her wishes unmet, but they could not be met, they had no limit. The story absolved Nat, who couldn't love her mother enough, but there was not enough love in the world for that.

She mixed the dough for the buns and thought of Felix and that she, much more than her mother, was the Fisherman's Wife, standing in her transformed kitchen, kicking out at her fortunate life (why hadn't Frankie texted? She should have by now), braced for disaster, agonizing over Felix's unhappiness. Maybe Frankie was right (she wouldn't tell her that) and he was normal, ordinary, and why did she think that she, of all the people in the world, deserved that her children would be spared ordinary suffering? Who was she, or her children, to be spared everything?

But what if she'd ignored all the signs? That was a theme in the stories Nat found on her phone: the parents or the wife or very rarely the husband who had ignored the signs. *He was so quiet. You couldn't have guessed.* She was fascinated by the stricken parents, insisting they had no idea, until the building had burned, the girl was dead, the rifle had been concealed in a knapsack, or something much less (of course less, what was wrong with her?) yet unbearable, the young man who sifted through incendiary message boards in the middle of the night and slept through the day, in an upstairs room forever, having missed his only life. Nat thought there was something wanting, something remiss, in the parents she read about. Surely they were at fault. They ought to have known.

When Nat's grandmother died (after a fall down the stairs, a long fading-out in hospital, nothing like the old woman smoking in her chair), Nat had an important exam and didn't help for the first week. She arrived to find her mother and Nick taping up cardboard boxes, the house half-dismantled, sheets pulled off the bed, the blinds torn from the windows. It looked like a house under siege, the inhabitants grabbing whatever they could. Nat thought of her grandmother as a starved young girl, running from German soldiers. She'd eaten the dog, then shoe leather, then grass.

The picture of the road and the trees was gone, and Nat didn't ask about it. Nick was furious at being left to deal with their mother alone.

'You could have waited for me.'

'Really? You think I can make her wait?'

They paused in their standoff, listening to their mother in the basement flinging cans into a bin to give to the food bank (but the food bank wouldn't take them, too dented, too old), working with a manic urgency as if she could outpace her inconvenient grief.

Nat looked at the spot on the wall where the painting had hung and forgot it was her grandmother she had lost, devastated by the loss of the painting's evening light. Nick, sighing at her uselessness (he was apprenticing to an electrician; like their mother, he thought her life was a judgment on his), went upstairs to check the water pressure in the shower.

In the university library she'd lift down art books with their coated paper, their stately covers in fading cloth stamped with gold. Each time she'd hope but she never found the picture, though she found many like it, yet nothing that reminded her enough of that light, that space and terror and beauty, a vastness opening and closing at the same time. Walking the streets of different cities throughout her life, she would be transfixed by the angle of the light, usually in winter or spring, stretching over unfamiliar houses. Frankie would ask her what she was thinking, and she tried to describe the painting and failed to convey what it meant. Just a road at dusk, some trees.

Frankie kissed the corner of her mouth, shortly after the exam, Nat flushed with her success and the clarity of loss, which made her want to change her life.

Frankie did manage to finish her PhD, though it had nothing to do with her eventual job, running the HR department of a large business school. Nat faltered in her scholarship, sidetracked by beautiful useless things, drawn to the obscure and the irrelevant.

She failed in her analysis, less excited by arguments about reading than by reading itself. She grew bored with densely printed texts pointing out phallic symbols or female defilement. The play of language was more interesting than the meaning she could coax from it. She collected trinkets like a bird carrying oddments to a nest, ghost stories and folk tales and fustian poems, rescuing these things from the totalizing coherence of theory. Her abandoned thesis was on Christina Rossetti, a religious lady poet who composed glorified nursery rhymes, best remembered for the lyrics to a carol (*snow had fallen, snow on snow, snow on snow, in the bleak midwinter, long ago*), unable to marry because she and the stammering man she loved could not agree on the nature of God. Nat, surprised by her own existence, getting fisted on her threadbare sheets and sleeping till noon, working at the university library and waiting for Frankie to get off shift at the restaurant, loved Rossetti's earnestness, her lost-cause life. She kept a photograph on her desk of Rossetti, shrunken in her bonnet, confronting the camera with fanatical pale eyes.

O where are you going with your love-locks flowing
On the west wind blowing along this valley track?
The downhill path is easy, come with me an it please ye,
We shall escape the uphill by never turning back

She tried to find a queer reading, a post-colonial reading, a feminist reading, a hint of something correctly radical in this modest melancholy body of work, but she just liked the rolling rhythm of the words on the page. It was the rhythm of walking, of walking along a street at dusk and noticing the light and wondering what had happened to the painting, and why awe and dread are the same thing. She liked the danger in the poem, the young woman calling to the figure who passes by and invites her to come with him though the road opens into hell, and by the time she realizes where he is leading her, there is no way back. The chaste Rossetti had no mercy in her, no true forgiveness.

She should have stuck with it, Nat thought on the increasing days when she wondered why she hadn't done more. Teased something out: the demon-lover ballad tradition, female perversity, something like that. Nat was very interested in the possibilities of perversity, in that heady short period before her life had become domestic and socially acceptable even to her mother. Marriage, house, children. It was feasible for her mother to overlook Frankie, to regard her as an appendage, which was what husbands were anyway. Her mother congratulated herself on her tolerance, which Frankie did not seem to mind.

Frankie did not seem to miss, either, the shimmer of transgression that had hovered over their lives, as Nat often did. It had felt like freedom. Thinking of what had become possible within her lifetime, she felt slightly cheated, as if previous generations, with their furtive fear of exposure, were more authentic than she was, so settled in her ordinariness. And she knew it was a good trade; on balance she would rather have her marriage (which Frankie had insisted on, crying through the ceremony) recognized, her rights to her children protected. Bedside tables piled with books, school schedules on the fridge, dinner parties. She was just old enough for it to seem improbable that she would have children, a marriage, that her name and Frankie's would appear together on the documents of their house, on all the paperwork that trailed behind them, showing their establishment in the world. Sometimes she caught herself expecting that someone would object, as if she were the punchline of a long drawn-out joke and would be revealed as foolish, a grand folly, to have believed her life was acceptable. She could not explain (there was no clear way to explain, no one had asked for an explanation) that she kept thinking she must be mistaken, to have believed her life was solid and defended. It could not be real.

She set the dough on the table to rise, covered it with a dampened towel.

The poem, of course, is also about the horror of the mistake that does not seem costly until after it is made. Middle-aged, crow-footed, her belly folding over, she stood in her kitchen and let herself be overtaken by her son's sadness, his loss, which she should have prevented, and she did not know what loss she meant, he was not lost, why must she think he was lost?

O where are you going with your love-locks flowing
On the west wind blowing along this valley track?

Afternoon

The rats are hiding.

In the middle of the day they retreat into their new tunnels, keep their eyes on the water from a safe distance. The sound of water fills their ears. They sniff the soaked earth.

As the water rises, the sump pump shudders, expelling through a black hose that leads up through the hole at the front of the house and to the sidewalk, running across and into the street to the storm drain.

When the hole was dug, growing larger each day, they were uneasy, the maw gaping with light. Now they are used to it.

The rats regard the sump pump, noting the threatening motion it makes.

A rat will live anywhere there is water. Like humans, they are destructive and everywhere, their only constant a proximity to rivers and streams.

Here they have a river in the dark.

The pump works mightily but not successfully.

They will live here as long as there is a river. It is their river.

The walls of the basement are swollen, the back wall shored up with cinderblocks. The cinderblocks will wear, given time. The front wall is much older, the stones weeping through the uneven chinks in the masonry.

The sun hits the hole at the front of the house and reaches in, down across the water, which is full of grey and brown clots of earth. The rats can't see the bottom. The light reflects back onto the support beams below the main floor.

Outside, a human foot wearing a heavy boot shifts a piece of plywood over the hole, so the light comes in only at the edges. The rats, glad of the darkness, smell smoke. They twitch in their hiding places.

She could find the phone in her pocket, but she needed to think about how to get up. If she called Bobby, that would be the end. *Ma! Ma! Don't be scared! Don't move! I'm coming.* She'd go into the box.

Stretching her left hand, she patted the coat she'd brought down from the hook, grabbing at it as she reached the bottom. Her long black coat, with the lumpy packet of lemon candies so she wouldn't cough in church, but that church was gone now, there was a new glass church. Her old church was condos.

If Bobby knew she was lying at the foot of the stairs, she would have to sell the house, he would make her, he would begin his speeches about *what is best.* She wouldn't let him win. He couldn't trick her into one of the coffin boxes. She would never tell him. Even with the pain, she grunted at her upper hand.

The pain was so clear, so sharp, a radiant knot around her hip. The shock of the fall had jolted her bladder, the wet housedress plastered around her thighs. The smell. If she could get up before Gabriel came home, she could get to the sink, wash out the dress. Not be found shamed at the bottom of the stairs.

Turning her head, she could see the front door's rectangle of yellow glass. She would catch Gabriel's shadow when he came home, she'd learned to watch for his shadow and judge his state by how long it took for him to open the door. He drank with those men. His father would not have looked at them. Gabriel gave them cigarettes and they gave him beer and he came home and groaned on the couch.

Wet. She drew her hands slowly down her body, over the flat of her chest where her breasts used to be, avoiding the stain at her thighs, thought of the bruise that would rise along her side, dark as a grape skin. Grapes in the backyard, she'd made her own wine from them. The grapes bursting like organs, thin blood coating her fingers. Her mother and father grew grapes too, a long time ago.

Maybe she wasn't hurt. On TV a man didn't know he was hurt until he felt his head (she touched her hair), the pool spreading around him like a speech bubble. Comic books with speech bubbles, read ragged. Bobby's collection was still in the basement. She felt around her ears. Dry.

The driftwood of her arms and legs, everything drooping and turning in on itself. As a child she'd gathered crabs in a bucket of water and seen, scattered along the beach, the broken dead crabs picked by gulls, the threads of parched flesh mixed with sand. She'd left her parents. It was too far away to visit. She had sent her parents money. Bobby used to remind her that he took care of her better, he didn't understand. He thought the world had nothing in it he didn't understand. He didn't go to church. She had failed.

If she could get up before Gabriel came home, he wouldn't tell Bobby.

She couldn't move.

The pain was like glass, like ice.

She opened the front of the housedress, felt along her ribs, her hip. Her skin was whole. Her skin would grow so thin before she died that she would be able to see her own organs, the way she'd seen Gabriel's organs when he was born, his skin stretched wax, he shone blue and red, she was afraid of him, he might tear. She was not allowed to touch him.

She sat beside the incubator, watching his newborn eyes hurt by the light, pressing her palms against the plastic box. She didn't believe he would survive, so she mourned him.

When they took him home, she didn't know how to want him. The beating of his small heart. His lungs those paper balloons from childhood that she'd made out of newspaper and filled with water to throw at her enemies. He didn't belong to her.

If she hadn't been afraid of him, would his life have been different? But she was afraid, like he came from another place, like a movie with aliens. A person goes away somewhere and comes back carrying something inside them. He liked those movies. There was something inside him. She hoped she died before she knew what it was. She hoped she was not dying now. With the two of them stuck together in the house, she had come too close to knowing what was inside him. God would call him Gabriel.

Sometimes she wished God would call him. He would do something terrible, she didn't know what, but something. She would come in from the kitchen and serve him dinner and watch his face as he watched TV, his wolf's face, and know that in time he would show what was inside him, and she wouldn't be able to escape knowing. It would be her fault, this thing inside him. Everyone knew the worst things were the mother's fault. She knew it. He would show himself. When he was younger, she expected a knock on the door, police, a photograph of a woman or a child (not a child, please not a child). Now she thought of a gun in a mall, a car driven into a crowd. One day he would not come back from his walk, she would watch the light through the bubbled yellow glass. Waiting for a knock, hearing a knock. Officials, uniforms.

She would not get up yet. If she was hungry, she could eat the candies from the coat pocket. If only she had some water.

Maddy would decorate the tart with thinly sliced berries and powdered sugar after it cooled. The kitchen smelled of toasted almonds. Milo had stuck his fist into the bag of icing sugar and the table was covered, the lid of the butter dish, the trivet she'd set ready for the tart when she took it out of the oven. She yelled at him. He ran upstairs.

Someone should apologize before piano. She heard him talking to himself in his room. Should she apologize? If someone must, it would probably have to be her.

She hesitated at the bottom of the stairs, trying to catch words. He seemed untroubled, as if he'd forgotten. Should she apologize?

Her house trembled from the house next door, whatever the man was working on. Her house was made of cardboard. Nat quoted a poem once, *some women marry houses*, but Maddy didn't remember the rest and didn't read poetry. She wasn't married to her house, that was hurtful, Nat knew or should have, but she listened closely to her house, the creaks and bangs, the settling.

Sometimes, not at night when Alex worked late, this would have frightened her, but in the daytime, she sensed the house tuning itself in concert with other noises, the old dog barking on the porch, the cars surmounting the bridge over the railway tracks, a siren a long way off. She was part of a concert, her movements and her tasks (she placed her phone on the dining room table and went back to her kitchen, she wouldn't look) a thrum in the whole. Her house, her street, her neighbourhood, this city where she had lived the first half of her life (less, surely less, she wasn't middle-aged, not yet), was listening to itself and pacing itself in ways she would never understand and yet was part of. She mustn't wreck her life; there was so much she would destroy.

But at night, when thinking about the concert of the house was too close to believing in ghosts, when Alex worked late, she remembered herself memorizing Shakespeare, an exercise in which students were instructed to repeat a passage aloud over and over until the meaning, which came from the torque of the language itself, showed through. She had stayed up all night, her roommates at a party, saying the words like a spell, and meaning kept emerging, it was painful like the kick of a drill jarring your whole body. Like finding something inside rock. She pictured herself alone in her room with the force of a fantasy to lull her into sleep. As if that solitary person, learning to obliterate themselves, learning to vanish, was truer than this person, attuned to her house. She'd never thought she'd have a house. Alex was the reason she had a house. She was grateful. He deserved more than her gratitude, and the dislike that came after it. There was nothing wrong with him.

Her phone bloomed and she ran to it. Just an email about a parent council meeting, and she shouldn't have run, her agent wouldn't email. She stopped at the dining room table, looked up at the hanging lamp, a present from Alex, who'd seen her admire it in the store window on their date night, white lacquered paper stretched over wire ovals, shading the circle of Edison bulbs, Alex was so thoughtful, so extravagant, and she loved the frail flutter of the lamp, like aspen leaves.

She pictured the house divided, the lamp unhooked, the shade listing to one side. Herself in an apartment somewhere that Alex would pay for, but everything was so expensive now, it would be a concrete box where she would patch together her life. Go out with her old friends and commiserate, and be the same as they were. Adaptable, clinging to the barest chances. Making it through with gritted teeth and want.

The house kept shaking. Going back to the kitchen, she lifted the biggest jars down from the shelf on the shared wall, the vibrations nudging them toward the edge. Her kitchen spangled with glass, grains of rice like a wedding, flour billowing over her. Her tart ruined, her kitchen ruined. The young man next door unconcerned, not meeting her eyes. She was as angry as if it had actually happened.

She would pull the man into her house and show him what he'd done, the glass sticking out of the dessert, a cut, yes, a bad cut on Milo's foot, she'd lift Milo's small pink foot and show him the red sickle from the glass shard. The man would tell her it was her fault for storing such large jars on such a narrow shelf. She was so angry now. It was disappointing that her kitchen looked the same.

Or perhaps he'd be contrite, ashamed. Horrified by his own carelessness. How could he wreck everything so thoughtlessly? She'd seen that in him, a capacity for sorrow, for remorse. He would be bowled over, stand apologizing in her kitchen, barely able to get words out, like earlier on the sidewalk. She allowed herself (feeling silly, but it was fine if no one knew) to imagine tears in his eyes, at her anger and her righteousness (the cut on Milo's sweet foot) and of course his turmoil at how often he thought of her, how beautiful he thought she was. Unless he hadn't noticed, unless no one noticed anymore? She used to take it as her due. That would be over soon. She'd wasted it, wasted everything. The young man stood in her kitchen, in tears. She was so embarrassed now. She didn't care. He was in her kitchen in tears, looking like a humiliated boy. There was glass everywhere.

She tried to remember the last time Alex cried. She thought maybe when Milo was born, but she couldn't remember.

The noise stopped.

She looked down at the perfect tart and willed her phone to ping. Now, in this moment, when she was not looking, now would be the good news, when her life changed.

She went to her phone and glanced at it casually. Nothing.

In the silence she could hear Milo again, making up a story. In his stories he was always the hero, scoring the goal, singing the hit song, narrating his own triumph. If he caught her listening, he went quiet, smiling to himself, not abashed but waiting for her to stop. He wanted his secrets.

Today she sensed a particular secret, a plan. She wouldn't ask. She wanted to be the kind of mother who let her children have secrets.

The noise came back.

She hadn't seen Sylvie all day. They must still be in the schoolyard. Sitting scornfully on a bench, Sylvie's scorn imitative, adjusting herself to what Clio demanded. Heads bent together, long thin arms and legs decorated with bracelets, temporary tattoos. Sylvie scratched at the puckered skin of her elbows, raising white lines, blood. Maddy assumed she must be allergic to something, the lavender hand soap in the bathroom, but the dermatologist said no. And Maddy knew it was because of Clio, worse when Clio was there. Clio was a bully, and Nat, who talked about power all the time, didn't notice. Only Maddy saw the pain in the way Sylvie hung her head, listening for whatever Clio wanted to tell her, her whole body braced for Clio. Begging wordlessly not to be left.

When Maddy tried to ask about Clio, Sylvie was outraged, told her she was making stuff up, it wasn't Clio's fault she scratched too hard. Well, Sylvie wanted her secrets too. Everyone wanted secrets. Milo's secrets brought him joy, that's all, and Sylvie's didn't.

One for sorrow, two for joy, three for a girl, and four for a boy.

Maddy had sung that in a movie, a twee folk horror that had done unexpectedly well, but she was only in one scene, implicitly supernatural in a green dress, singing at the top of a flight of stairs with one hand over her mouth so the words could barely be heard.

Five for silver, six for gold, seven for a secret never told.

Maddy adopted it as a song for Sylvie's long bedtimes, holding her daughter's knobby body in the bed she would rise from, screaming, in the middle of the night. The tune was pretty.

Devil, devil, I defy thee. Devil, devil, I defy thee.

One night Sylvie, rigid in the darkness under the phosphorescent stars dotting her ceiling, asked Maddy to never sing it again. It frightened her.

Of course it frightened her. What was the secret?

Maddy knew that each character must have a secret. She pondered important secrets even when only in a single scene, singing a nursery rhyme. It was exciting to think about everyone having a secret. Wondering about the secret, guessing the secret.

Her secrets seemed trite. She might not love her husband, she wanted the young man to find her beautiful, she was afraid her life was dissolving, that she hadn't got hold of her life, what did that mean, how did you get hold of your life or lose the thread of it? But those were not worthy secrets. Following herself through the grocery store, she would have thought no, no, not that, that woman needs more than that, deserves more than that, she must have a secret that is deeply buried, ruinous, something she can barely bring herself to think and can never say.

Last night Alex worked late. Maddy got herself a bowl of ice cream. She would eat it in front of her laptop, cross-legged on the bed in what was officially a guest room but which she often asked Alex to sleep in, she liked to read late and he left early. Some days she barely saw him, half waking to hear him tiptoeing downstairs, drinking his coffee at the sink, not blending his smoothie so he wouldn't disturb his family. She would eat the ice cream and look at that article Nat sent about performance in the age of #MeToo, no, she would ignore the article, Nat was always sending articles she thought might interest Maddy, but Maddy wanted to look at things Nat pretended to despise: lists of beautifying antioxidants, best-dressed celebrities, photographs of the interiors of marvellous houses perched on the edges of cliffs or by the sea, the houses of famous gay men and their adopted or surrogate-birthed twin daughters in wonderful yellow dresses, the family grouped around a statement table made of granite, where they ate layered green things prepared by a personal chef. They made teasing conversation, washed in the light from the sea-facing wall, all glass. And she loved reading lists online: what to do, what not to do, what to think, unfolding instructions in black on ivory showing her what was right, how marriage ought to feel, how to ensure a happy childhood. Sometimes Maddy looked at lists of which celebrities were queer (that word again, she had trouble saying it aloud), she'd tell Nat, but Nat never knew who any of the people were, so she wasn't very interested and she said it was neo-liberal, without explaining why.

She was about to take a bite when Milo called her upstairs. She hid the bowl behind the open laptop so Sylvie wouldn't see it if she went to use the bathroom. She would demand some, Milo would run downstairs, and the three of them would end up on the couch watching that show where miniaturists competed to design the best dollhouse, one of the only things they agreed on. Furniture and books and tea sets and blankets and pillows, tiny and exquisite, a life you could grasp and contain, fitted into your cupped hands.

Upstairs, she got in the bed beside Milo.

'Did you have a nightmare?'

'No. I just wanted you.'

She had held Milo, smelled his sour hair. Downstairs, the ice cream was becoming watery, with little islands of fat. That was as far as she allowed her thoughts to go. She would not reveal any secrets. She had nothing to reveal. But she wanted a secret, her life was supposed to be the scaffolding around a secret, that was what a life was.

She called Milo downstairs to leave for his lesson, chivvied him out the door. The jars intact on kitchen table. Nothing had happened, nothing would happen.

The woman ran out of the house after her son, the little boy's cape lifting in the wind as he reached the corner and let her catch him. Together they leapt over the stream of water from the hose. The underside of the cape glittered red, the frayed edges unravelling from the gold outer layer. They turned the corner and were gone. She hadn't looked at Ilya.

Ilya looked at the spot where she'd turned. The man with the dragging foot came into view, drunkenly swaying up the stairs to his mother's house but stopping halfway. Ilya remembered him from church, the day he'd almost gone with Simon. The man, changing his mind, climbed back down the steps. He nodded at Ilya, an inept attempt at masculine reflex, showing they were not enemies. Straightening, he set off in the same direction as the woman and the boy, his left hand scattering something invisible behind him into the road.

When Ilya had seen the man at church, he was washed and combed. His neck flashed between the wispy hair and the shirt collar, white as a dried fish. Standing outside, Ilya watched through the windows. The man took his place at the back, his head lifted to the floating cross suspended on wire, made of the same cheap laminate as the pews.

The man moved lightly back and forth, as if stirred by a wind, and to Ilya he looked like holiness, something Ilya was not allowed to have. The preacher, bulky in his blue suit, sprang up the steps to the pulpit. Then the inner doors were shut, and Ilya, left on the sidewalk, could see only the vestibule, the pale green carpet, and the walls decorated with prints of a pastel Mary at the manger and the risen Christ, his heart a valentine.

The church was near the ruined house. Not like the few churches of Ilya's childhood (his family went only for weddings, baptisms), dark places made of stone, sleepy with incense. A square glass-fronted beige building Ilya passed on his way to buy pizza from the cheap place on the corner across from the supermarket. The congregants meagre in a space that could have easily held five hundred, but there were usually only a few dozen, the women in too-large blouses, the men in slippery suits. Ilya thought they left the door propped open till the sermon began so the passersby would feel their separateness, but Simon insisted the doors were open to show that anyone was welcome, all should enter and be born again.

Simon asked him to come to church with him after months of working side by side on the house, complaining about the owner's stupidity as they heaved the buckets of wet earth and watched the water rise in the basement. Ilya offered cigarettes, and Simon managed to say he didn't smoke or drink without sounding self-satisfied. Ilya promised he would come to church, liking the friendly way Simon asked, as if he were impulsively inviting Ilya for a beer. Ilya didn't tell Simon about his accident or that this was his first job after leaving his sister's house, but Simon understood that Ilya had worked much larger jobs, that gutting a house for an erratic opportunist was more than Ilya was worth. Simon too: he operated cranes, but the job came through a friend of his uncle, a stopgap until he could legally work. Like Ilya, he was paid in cash.

Ilya knew Simon wouldn't stay. He had plans. He lived with his uncle, sent money to his parents in Nairobi, said a short prayer before he ate or picked up his tools. Like refusing cigarettes, he did this without ostentation. Simon noticed the scars on Ilya's hands but didn't ask. Ilya hoped that someday Simon would ask. Ilya would tell. He wanted Simon to know.

Simon looked up from Ilya's hands and said that God was everywhere and in everything and that Ilya should talk to God. It was easy. God was in the world. The devil also. You knew the devil by his false face. Ilya wondered if Simon pictured a particular face, an enemy. The lawyer's office, the widows. There were no accidents. The relief of good and evil, of God or the devil in everything. Ilya was jealous of Simon, thinking Simon was not lonely in the way Ilya was.

Ilya arrived early. He didn't have a suit, and wore dark jeans and a clean black shirt, hoping Simon wouldn't be offended. He saw Simon in the parking lot, chatting with other men. He was dressed in a grey suit. Ilya wondered what on earth he himself was doing there. He wondered the same about Simon, in this congregation that was otherwise Portuguese or Brazilian, young couples gripping the hands of reluctant children. What did the old Catholic parents think of their children, their grandchildren, choosing this evangelical embrace?

He didn't go inside. At the house the next day, he didn't explain. Simon didn't ask him again.

Ilya moved the hose, breaking the ribbon of water, pulling the hose as far as it would go, the nozzle almost at the sewer, where the woman had turned without looking at him. The water, drawn up from the basement by the pump, was disarmingly clear, like something you could drink.

Simon had described baptism, his head pushed under the water, opening his eyes to the light breaking above him, trying to remind himself he was not drowned but saved, the preacher's hands holding him under long enough to let him feel salvation, the returning air opening his lungs.

Ilya thought about the minister's hands forcing all those heads underwater, and the woman not turning back, how she tangled her hair in her hands, what her hands would feel like.

The water twisted over itself, gathering dust and Ilya's cigarette butts and the yellow shreds of a chocolate wrapper.

Simon stopped coming to work. Maybe he got deported, maybe he found a better job, one that would lead to a life where he could make plans, where he didn't need to dwell on false faces. Or maybe he'd quit in disgust with the owner, with the disaster of the house. Ilya couldn't ask; no one in the crew knew.

In Ilya's mind and sometimes in his dreams, Simon fell from a scaffold, too late to grab the rope, turning as the ground rose up to claim him. Ilya searched his phone for reports of accidents at construction sites in Toronto, then nearby cities, then towns. The plain wooden cross Simon had worn streaming in the wind as he fell, the chain twisting in the air like the stream of water in the gutter.

He pulled at the hose, dislodging the last shred of the chocolate wrapper. He put one hand behind him, imitating the motion of throwing something away, the same motion the man had made, rounding the corner. Ilya remembered what it reminded him of, a painting a high school teacher had tacked up in a corner, showing a man sowing a field, as if these bored city children would be interested in a French peasant from the nineteenth century flinging seeds from a bag slung across his body. Ilya was interested; it was something to look at when he wasn't listening (he sat at the back all through high school, he never said a word). The arc of the sower's arm, the certainty of a repeated motion, the body that knows, through work, what it means. The muttering man's arm seemed as sure as the sower's, convinced of what he did, like Ilya had been before he fell.

Ilya sometimes went as far as the door of the church. At first he believed he might find Simon there. When he understood he would not see Simon ever again, he tried to force himself to go inside. He would testify, he would believe in the mercy of God, he would kneel and be blessed, the preacher would press his hands to Ilya's forehead, showing Ilya that it was possible to be touched.

Felix quickened, following. He could see the walking man up ahead, that motion he made with his fingers like he was throwing something behind him. This was it, at last. Following the man, he was a spy.

He'd almost gone home again, trailing around the neighbourhood, walking further than he was allowed, toward Queen Street. Nothing anywhere. A few people he knew, and adult strangers looking at phones, but nothing interesting. A dead rat, guts open, under the railway bridge. He saw some boys from school, stopped to say hi. Nat thought he didn't know anyone, he could hear Nat and Frankie arguing about it sometimes. (Did they think he couldn't hear them? He heard everything they said.) He kept walking; he didn't have much to say to those boys. But he knew them, he knew people. Nat acted like he didn't know anyone, just because he wasn't like Clio, who needed Sylvie to send heart emojis when she took a shit. He put his earbuds in. The world blurred with music, echoing the thud of his footsteps. He let his hair fall into his eyes, liking how the sun turned prismatic through the strands. A cloud around him. Nat said she didn't want him to disappear into his phone, but he wished he could disappear. Become a coil of white smoke, a pure loop of sound. Heavy metal pulsing like a heart about to explode.

He'd avoided the schoolyard where Clio and Sylvie swapped useless secrets. He'd heard his parents talking about the classmate, those drawings Clio and Sylvie left in her desk, and Frankie thought the principal made too big a deal out of it, the drawings weren't violent. Nat thought they should send Clio to a therapist, but Clio was good at explanations and could talk herself out of anything, and the principal said people liked her. The principal liked Clio; the principal was Clio. She smiled at Felix over her desk, clicking her silver pen, pretending she liked him, but she only liked people like herself. She used the word *help* a lot, and *strategy* and *mental health*. Strategies meant he had to do what she wanted while pretending that wasn't what she was asking. Clio would be like that, clicking a pen and smiling like a horror movie, the woman in the nice white dress but you look inside her mouth and there are rows and rows of teeth going way down into the swallowing squelching dark. Bitch. He knew this was a forbidden word (even Frankie grew stern, and she was hard to piss off). He kept a list of words like that in the back of a notebook. Words that rip the world open.

He liked the possibility of the world ripping open. Better than everything always going on the same. That was why he liked to collect jokes (sometimes he told them to classmates, he was actually pretty good at making them laugh at the wrong times, that was why the principal clicked her pen at him, he wouldn't stop, he got angry when he was told to stop). A good joke, a really funny joke, especially a joke about the wrong thing, was another way of ripping the world open. Like knowing what was inside the principal's mouth. That snort of laughter when it hits, you can't help yourself, you are carried away. The joke saves you from everything going on exactly the same.

He'd stood watching the dog on the porch for a while, hoping the dog would come down the steps. The rope was long enough for that. The dog had been there as long as he could remember, but he still didn't know the dog's name. The dog knew him, he should know the dog's name.

'Hi! Hi, boy!'

The dog looked up, wriggling his tail and back legs, a polite motion before he went back to his task. The rope was frayed to a few coarse strands.

When he saw the walking man up ahead, he took out his earbuds. Stay sharp, stay close, but not so close that he couldn't melt away unseen.

The walking man grumbled to himself. Felix followed. Left, right, left again, then right again down the short street to the east of the house with the hole in front, the dead-end street that stopped at the fence to the train tracks.

Felix liked this place. Vines grew up and along the fence, hiding the gap where someone had clipped the links. Sometimes Felix ducked through the gap when no one was watching, carefully because the clipped ends were sharp, they could draw blood. Sat with his back to the fence and waited for a train. Small stones in his hand. He'd throw them at the train windows, imagining the passengers startled by the plink against the glass. Looking up, wondering what was happening.

At the fence the man stopped, and Felix thought he was about to climb over. The man didn't know about the gap. He'd take off his shirt to throw over the loops of razor wire at the top, like that YouTube video about how to break into construction sites. Felix watched it over and over, so many times he could feel the movements in his limbs, his body remembering what he hadn't done. If the man climbed over the fence, he'd follow him.

The man turned back so quickly Felix jumped, hid behind a concrete pole. The man was almost running. Felix trotted after him, the way they'd come, past the dog again and down the alley. He wasn't allowed to walk in the alley alone, or to follow the man, this was like writing words in the back of his notebook, writing down the jokes he knew enough not to say aloud.

The walking man stopped at the far end of the alley. Felix slowed, creeping. He thought about trying to scare him, to see what would happen. The man kept muttering, but it was focused now, purposeful. He was trying to do something, only half-hidden by the straggling trees that had seeded themselves in the thin line of earth where the alley turned right toward another street. The man sighed and Felix watched the impressive yellow arc, the pool gathering in the dust and breaking off in rivulets, following the cracks. That was it. Ordinary after all.

She would go home soon. It was too late to get a rope at the hardware store. She giggled softly: not too late, just too much beer. There was that boy, out by himself again. His shirt was dirty and his hair too long, falling greasy in his eyes. If she had a kid, she'd take better care of him than that. She'd make sure her kid had a clean shirt, not let him out looking like a fucking orphan. Maybe he'd smile once in a while.

For a second, she'd thought she saw the shadow in the bubbled yellow glass, but it vanished again. Nothing. Could she call out, yell until someone in the street heard her? But the roar from the young man's tools had started again, and the music, and her mouth felt too dry for sound. She was so thirsty. In a minute she would try to get up. Any minute now. Any minute.

It was time to find Clio and Sylvie. Nat looked away from the men on the porch as she passed Maddy's street, on to the schoolyard. She saw Felix coming out of the alleyway and pretended not to, letting him lope toward her and follow behind, as if that was his plan all along. She wouldn't mention the alley, one of the forbidden places like the train tracks and the old fieldhouse roof in the park on the other side of the bridge. If only Frankie could witness Nat's restraint. She'd left her phone on the counter in an act of self-disciplined virtue, she would not check or send anything, and as a reward, there would be a message from Frankie apologizing, and praising her. She felt better. Look, she had left him alone, she had let him be, like Frankie wanted. That didn't mean Frankie was right.

She waited for him at the fence, watching the girls on the bench in the empty playground. Their hands covered in that white dust. They'd sat on the bench exchanging pebbles when their legs didn't reach the ground; at ten, there was a half-ironic nostalgia to how they sat, the way girls that age would use the swings, shrieking and leaning back in a caricature of their earliest childhood, so no one would think they meant it.

Sylvie's wounded eagerness was so like Maddy's. It made sense that Clio was planning her exit. Clio was ruthless; Nat guessed Sylvie was betrayed in small ways any time someone more interesting came into view. Clio would get what she wanted, and would know what it was without the obfuscation of guilt. This would come in handy later, when there would be scorched earth and famine, and it would be necessary to fight over scraps of food and dirty water. Clio would survive. Sylvie would be eaten. Clio would eat her.

Nat sometimes made lists in her head of who would survive and who would be eaten. This was okay if she never told anyone, certainly not Frankie, who might not understand it was a joke. It was a joke. She hoped.

Felix caught up to her, grasped the chain-link fence, and rattled. 'Come on! Get up!'

She jumped at how loudly he yelled, how authoritatively.

The girls ignored him.

'Why don't you go get them?' Nat asked. 'Maybe they can't hear you.'

'They can *hear* me.'

This was Felix's school too, since kindergarten. In June he would leave it for middle school, an event he seemed to treat with indifference, like a prisoner moving between identical cells, except to complain that he would have to take the bus. He was waiting out the present but not aspiring to anything that might replace it.

He'd always been difficult, but there had been passions. He'd taught himself to split wood at the rented cottage last summer, finding the hatchet in the tool shed, approaching the chopping block frowning, the tip of his tongue poking out from between his teeth the way Frankie's did when she was caught up in a task. Frankie, who'd grown up backwoods camping every summer, showed him how to hold the hatchet and went back into the house, blocking Nat at the door when she tried to run out, imagining the hatchet slipping, coming down on his foot.

Nat dug out her secret cigarettes and sat smoking on the deck, regretting it when Frankie described watching him through the kitchen window, his quiet confidence as he planted himself, driving the hatchet down the centre of the log. He'd built up their fires in the evenings, shining with accomplishment. Even Clio was impressed, glancing up from the armchair where she'd settled with a cardboard box of horror novels she'd found under the bed.

These books were inhabited by leather-faced men creeping down country roads to lonely houses, no help for the women and children eating their dinners inside. Nat warned Clio she would scare herself sick, but she read dispassionately, sometimes flipping to the end to see who survived and who didn't. Nat knew she should worry about Clio, but Clio would make it through (the horror novel, the apocalypse). Clio the Final Girl. Clio had explained patronizingly to Nat about Final Girls, most appearing in movies Clio was explicitly not allowed to watch and watched at friends' houses anyway (not Sylvie's house, Sylvie scared easily, but Clio was widely liked, an advantage she had over Sylvie, who wanted only Clio). Clio told Nat offhandedly, daring her to be angry. Nat always rose to the bait and regretted it afterwards.

Nat saw Clio swinging an axe over the body of the killer, her blood-spattered face grimly triumphant, floodlit in the beams from the too-late police cars skidding up the gravel drive. The flash of blue and red passing over the Final Girl's spent figure as she tosses off a quip, normalcy restored (until the sequel), represented by police sirens, the world of classic horror fundamentally conservative, reactionary (Nat knew she shouldn't lecture a child about politics, it was useless). Felix would be a shut-in, Clio a Final Girl. Nat would be eaten. She didn't know about Frankie. Frankie would make the best of it. Nat being eaten would be hard for Frankie, of course, but Frankie's innate cheerfulness would get her through.

Unless Felix wasn't a shut-in. Unless he was the man creeping down the dark roads. Jesus Christ. Stop it. Stop.

She marched into the schoolyard and hauled the girls up by their shirts.

Clio and Sylvie walked behind Nat, linking their pinkie fingers. The tight hook of Clio's finger felt like a promise to Sylvie. She pressed, promising back. She would do everything right. Behind them, Felix barely lifted his feet, scuffing his soles along the pavement, but she could feel his dislike, and it gave a definite shape to her and Clio, it made her lift her own feet higher, she swung Clio's hand bravely, and Clio actually smiled, not at her but because of her, Clio smiled, opening Sylvie's palm to the air, the long red thread of blood dry now, the skin beginning to knit. Clio was claiming her. Felix found one of the pebbles Clio had thrown over the fence, kicked it along. Nat wouldn't see anything.

Nat led Felix and the girls past the low wall, the ambiguous stretch of grass that belonged to the school but was used as a common space where young men drank, spilling over from the nearby parking lot, also the property of the school, also used as a gathering place, especially in the summers, when it crackled with a manic energy. The young men not bothering to hide their beer cans, indulging in showy unserious fights.

She remembered an argument with Alex, when the children were tiny. They were at a birthday party in the schoolyard, metallic balloons tied to the bench, the white-and-pink sheet cake melting in the sun, wasps buzzing over the bowls of chips and ignored grapes and woody carrots. Alex was irritably pained by the young men gathered around a car in the parking lot, music playing, shirts off. He wanted the young men to leave: it was school property, they were drinking, the children were daring each other to go over, some standing along the top of the wall, open-mouthed with admiration. She'd given a speech about sharing space and the importance of remembering that the young men came from households that had been here decades longer than hers or Alex's. The birthday party, the shrieking children, and the hostess archly pouring sangria into plastic cups for the parents, the piñata and the games and the streamers taped to the playground equipment, was as aggressively self-enclosed, as noisy, as the group of young men. Alex, with his creased forehead and reasonable doubts, was a puritan, yet Nat was embarrassed all the same, recalling her arms crossed over her chest, Alex stepping back, frowning in puzzlement, Maddy miserably silent. Frankie, of course, had wandered off deliberately, playing with the children, agreeing with Nat afterwards to keep the peace.

Nat was ashamed of the memory. She'd argued forcefully but didn't like the young men any more than Alex did. She never spoke to them; she wouldn't have known what to talk to them about.

The wall was full of messages, scrubbed away by the school a few times a year, always reappearing. Expansive graffiti, ordering the passersby to join various revolutions, become more aware, give land back, suck cock, love themselves, love the universe. Nat was fascinated by the care that had been taken, the shades of blue and gold and blood-red, the work of the middle of the night. She liked the stranger, smaller inscriptions, usually written in lurching black sharpie, single words, inside jokes, outrage directed at named people. Not a proclamation but a small thought, private yet important enough to leave on a wall.

She carried a cloth bag heavy with books. They would go to the library first, an Edwardian Arts and Crafts edifice with oblong windows curved at the top, double oak doors made of inlaid wood, evoking, she assumed, an imaginary England. Inside, the metal shelves and thin brown carpets of Nat's childhood, the overhead fluorescents mixing with the spring sunlight coming in through the glass, showing the dust motes.

She returned her books. The girls wandered in one direction, Felix in another. It was like herding cats. She found him on the second floor beside a man who was making a low growling noise. Felix stared at the man and licked his lips nervously, and Nat thought Felix wanted to speak to him. She wasn't sure if she was moved, thinking Felix wished to help the man, or alarmed that Felix was attracted to derangement, sensing in the man the desire for an enemy.

Overtaken by her habitual fears, she pictured Felix older, on the lookout for enemies, let herself believe he'd grasp at the possibility of an enemy in every word spoken to him. Someone behind a counter, a bus driver, a woman who asked him to move so she could push her stroller through a crowd. What if he learned to sense the man alone at the end of the bar, the man standing behind him in line, knowing how to catch the eye of the stranger whose instinct for self-preservation is less than their desire to fight? What if he wore his life lightly, something he wasn't sure he wanted to keep? What if the bartenders learned to watch closely when he came in, what if the woman walking alone at night crossed the street when she saw him, her gut telling her to be careful?

Stop it. Felix didn't get into fights. She didn't know who he would be. No one did, especially not Felix, staring at the man.

The growling continued, deep in the man's throat, like a dog. Did the man think he was a dog? Or wish he were? Dogs seem to attract more love than people do. A wet dribble ran from a sore inside one ear, down the red folds of the man's neck.

The library was a place that did not require payment or belief. People slumped into the chairs, surrounded by belongings in reusable plastic shopping bags striped in faded pink and blue, a few sitting on the floor, resting their heads against the heavier books, atlases, encyclopedias, books that no one used repurposed as furniture.

One old woman lay full-length at the end of the aisle, asleep, her arms wrapped around her bags. Other than the man making dog noises, the people among the books were silent, thinking of their own disasters. No, Nat thought, they could be thinking of the weather, which if you lived outside was not a passing thought, or imagining a winning lottery ticket, they could be thinking of the sun through the windows, the next drink or hit, or the volunteers who sometimes came with blankets, sandwiches in paper bags. Perhaps they listed their grievances, considered their enemies.

No one met her eyes. It must be exhausting to be so laid bare to the inconsequential compassion of strangers, their whims of pity.

Nat used to have theories of history. She had been well-versed in several theories, backed up with impressive examples and quotations. Now her theories seemed flattening, like the effects of literary theory on a poem. A game played by people like herself to pass the time. Theories of history were beside the point. The people were there.

Explaining them seemed to deny them substance, as if only she, with her training in theories of history, could understand. As if her understanding could mean anything to anyone's cumbersome life. And the theories were too obvious. They bored her. She bored herself; she was boring, she must be, to have so many theories. To have only an accumulation of vocabulary as her accomplishment in the world. To still, inevitably and without meaning to, be thinking of herself as she looked at the people. The theories were useless: looking, she was thrown back into her own experience, not theirs. It did not matter that she had theories. It mattered that she had property.

Nat put her hand on Felix's sleeve. They heard the girls squealing downstairs and the voice of the security guard at the front door telling them to be quiet. Maybe everything she imagined for Felix was wrong. They went downstairs together, her hand on his sleeve, and he allowed it.

Outside the girls followed behind. Nat wisely let go.

Felix tried to hear Sylvie and Clio. He didn't want them to know he was listening, dragged his feet so they would think he wasn't conscious of them, twittering softly. He found another stone, kicked it backward, hoping it would catch Clio's shin. The stone skittered into the road and they laughed. He wasn't sure if it was at him, but it must be, they would laugh at anyone who was there, better him than someone else. He could take it, he could take anything. He was going to be strong enough to take anything. A rush inside him, watchful excitement, thinking of growing strong enough to withstand any insult or injury. That new YouTube video about trials from long ago: you had to hold a red-hot iron in your hand, you had to carry it, that proved you were innocent, how long you could carry it. Lying in his bed watching, Felix looked from his phone to his hand holding it, the skin soft and folded around the lines of his palm. Wishing to be strong enough to let the metal burn into his skin. He could almost hear what Clio was saying. Or was it Sylvie? It was hard to tell in whispers.

The man's growling noise was in his own throat, rising inside him like the walking man's muttering or the dog, feebly menacing from inside his dreams. The wet dribble from the man's ear. The yellow arc in the alley, the words he wrote in the back of his notebook.

The girls kept whispering. He could almost catch what they said. He would protect the walking man and the man with the sore on his ear from them, he knew how dangerous the girls were. Nat had no idea. He was on his guard against all of them, and he was ready. Not afraid. He dug his fingernails into his palms. They would be surprised.

The sun bewildered Nat after the indoors. Felix was smiling, not at her but smiling, and they walked to the café. Passing people enjoying the day, and she couldn't refuse happiness because wretchedness existed. She should text Frankie, she should apologize, and she felt something opening inside like a fist going limp (though Felix's hands were clenched tight), entertaining the possibility that she was ridiculous, wrong about Felix, wrong about everything.

They went past that weird glass-walled evangelical church, past the photography studio, which today exhibited communion photographs, seemingly from the seventies or eighties, children in blue suits, white dresses, pressing Bibles to their chests, peering out from the brittle wings of their hair, the features of Jesus sorrowing in the background. Nat couldn't tell whether or not to take these pictures seriously, if they were a tribute to the Catholic stronghold of earlier times or a sneering joke, like hipster collections of votive candles. They went past the young man who played his saxophone in front of the pharmacy, and he bowed to them as if they had given him money, past the new store, which either sold fish or was an art gallery, Nat was genuinely unsure, past the health food store where Maddy bought expensive supplements that promised better skin, better guts, better nails, better concentration, better hair, better orgasms, better joy – Nat wanted these things too, but she made fun of Maddy for thinking she could buy them, for being frank about wanting them. They walked past neighbours Nat half knew and she smiled and they smiled, past the vandalized mailbox that was never replaced and past the awkwardly angled corner bench on which sat a metal sculpture of an avuncular dead philanthropist who had come from Italy, the plaque said, with nothing, and ultimately endowed a hospital.

Most of the time no one sat beside the dead metal man. The bench was the territory of the bird woman, who Nat could not stop thinking of as the bird woman; Clio and Sylvie, smaller, fascinated, called her that, and it was uncomfortably fixed in Nat's head, fitting the woman's swiftness.

The woman preferred not to sit on the bench but crouched in front of it, guarding her coins, which today were piled up in a small cardboard box, she must be having a good day, the warm weather opening wallets. Maria or Marianna (one was her and one was the old woman behind her curtains, Nat should be able to remember) bobbed her sharp-featured head, keeping up her monologue, a garble about her father and Yugoslavia, neither of which existed anymore.

The bird woman began to sing at the sight of them, something she did sometimes, a sustained high note, wordless but coming close to a word, like the opening of an aria. Nat thought she must have trained as a singer, in another life, somewhere else (Yugoslavia?), a life she barely remembered, clouded as she was. Unless it was the other way around, and the woman (Maria? Marianna?) experienced the past, Yugoslavia, her father, the cut-off note of the song, as sharply real. It was her present that was a fog.

The woman did not always panhandle, she also stalked this stretch of the intersection, ignoring the traffic lights, never getting hit (she did not dart but moved at a stately pace, lifting her legs high like a marionette), sidling close behind other walkers and vaulting into her one long note. People who were not familiar with her jumped. Nat had seen this happen several times; there was a slyness in the woman's face, as if she were in fact in total command of herself.

Nat thought someone must take care of her beyond the caseworker, imagining an estranged sibling, remembering her as she was before, whoever and wherever that had been. The woman was clean, and while her red hair showed inches of white at the roots, someone helped her from time to time to refresh the dye, and then it gleamed dark red, almost purple. The woman caressed it as she sang, her wrinkled skin more sallow when haloed by that garish red, but she was proud, she preened, gathering her shapeless brown sweater royally around her sunken chest. For a second she reminded Nat of Maddy, the red hair, the vanity, but Maddy could never be like this woman. Or this woman had never been like Maddy. But that was nonsense, this woman could have been very much like Maddy and Maddy could become this woman, in some unlikely but not impossible future.

The note again. The bird woman tilted back her head, her hands stretched over her cardboard box of coins. Behind Nat the girls whispered, and Felix, overhearing them, grimaced, half turned back, decided against it.

And then the café, which sold plants and handmade baby clothes and silkscreened greeting cards and wine as well as coffee. The baby clothes were made of cotton and felted wool, maroon and olive green, ochre and turquoise, and they were beautiful, not bunched along racks but on wooden hangers suspended from the ceiling with fishing twine. The breeze from the door opening made the nearest little dress dance, stirred the ruffles along the hem. The plants, also hanging from fishing line, were too heavy to move, trailing ivy and polished jade, nothing that flowered. Nat thought of affluent grandmothers buying the clothes, watching as the young woman wrapped them in silver tissue and placed them in brown paper bags.

The young woman performed her tasks gravely. Nat came here sometimes in the afternoons before school pickup, drank a coffee, half reading her book, half talking to the owner. Nat could see her in the back, adjusting the row of larger plants that sat in blue-glazed pots along a wooden shelf, partially visible through the thicket of baby clothes. The owner gave a curt wave, though her mouth tightened at the sight of the children, the girls loudly debating brownies and éclairs. But the young woman behind the counter smiled, and the girls looked down, so the smile went to Felix.

The owner had opened the café in a burst of optimistic rage after her divorce left her with money and time, and she had brought her niece from Japan to work for her. The niece had wanted an adventure or else she was a student here and worked for her aunt when she was not studying, Nat was not clear, perhaps it was a little of each.

Nat was slightly in awe of the owner, her commanding voice, the way she mocked herself for staying with her husband as long as she had, the way her mockery must conceal a shame so vast she could barely fathom it. *Everyone knew right away he was an asshole except me,* she had said, as if this was a casual thought, *but then we had kids and it was too late and then he left anyway*. After a pause, the woman had held out her phone and showed Nat a man's picture. *See?* And she pushed the phone into Nat's face, chuckling, *Look, there's the asshole.* When she said this, Nat thought she saw a flicker of deeper humiliation in the woman's face and wondered if the husband wasn't an asshole so much as a fool.

In the photograph a fair-haired man beamed with self-regard, holding up a glass, dressed in a suit he was too heavy for, but handsome, prosperous. It must have been a special occasion, perhaps an anniversary, the man standing in a large brilliant room full of people. He looked manically happy and fairly drunk, his mouth twisted in mid-sentence. It was a peculiar photograph to keep on a phone, to show to strangers. Keeping it must be cautionary, the woman reminding herself of her mistake. Perhaps she had watched him that night, wherever they were. Watched him hold forth and seen the looks on the faces of the listeners and realized he was a fool and everyone knew it, had always known it, except her.

The woman looked a little older than Nat, perhaps in her late fifties, her skin lucent with expensive attention, and she dressed in adult versions of the clothes she sold, wine-red sack dresses, brown linen jackets, her neck (she had a beautiful neck, withered like a milkweed pod) decorated with strings of glass beads or polished stones on silver chains. She wore many rings, as if to distract herself from the removed wedding ring. She was tender with her plants and curt with her niece. When the niece was not present, her aunt wondered aloud if she would stay, wondered who would replace her. Nat herself wondered why the woman spoke so freely, suspected a performance, wanting the people who came into the café to feel singled out. They had never exchanged names, and yet she knew enough about the woman's life to make a story.

Where did the woman fall on the list, Nat wondered. Would she survive or be eaten? Survive, she thought, but honourably. She would help others survive too. So what would she and Nat be to each other, when disaster came? If they found each other in the middle of a burning street, in the face of an advancing army, spotted one another clinging to flotsam in the flood, would they help one another? It was so hard to tell.

Disarmed by the woman, by the elegance of her smoothly arranged grey-threaded hair, Nat had told her about Felix's loneliness. She thought the woman's tightening mouth at the sight of the children was partly an acknowledgement of Felix, that she remembered everything. Nat blushed. She'd betrayed him. The woman hadn't betrayed anyone, except her ex-husband, who was fair game. She had barely mentioned her children. The niece was fair game too: anyone could see she was unhappy.

The niece stopped smiling, fell to polishing the knobs on the espresso machine. She too wore muted colours, greens and browns and blacks. Her English had improved, the aunt said, but Nat was not sure how, since she barely spoke. She was full of longing, Nat thought, having noticed her watching the younger people who came in, couples leaning into each other and asking questions about milk substitutes, women with their laptops meeting for work dates or starting businesses, Nat couldn't tell anymore, probably they were creating lifestyle brands or hoping to, speaking in conspiratorial voices, older versions of the mean girls Clio and

Sylvie were becoming. Nat imagined a tremor in one eye or in the corner of the girl's mouth as she pushed the blue-and-white saucers across the marble counter. Nat would have talked to her, but the girl was at a time in her life when a middle-aged woman did not concern her. Nat was not what she wanted. Nat was not what Felix wanted.

The children chose treats, and they crowded around a small table. Felix chewed with his mouth open, his hair in his eyes. His nails were dirty and needed cutting. Nat grew impatient as the girls competed for who could take the smallest bites, restrained herself when Clio, her eyes on Sylvie, stuck out her tongue and licked a single crumb from the sweet, ignoring Felix and Nat, ignoring everything, and (Clio ignored this too) Nat was surprised to hear a laugh from the niece at the counter, seeing them, but the laugh was cut off like the bird woman's note.

Clio suddenly changed the rules and swallowed the rest of her brownie, got up and left, pursued by Sylvie, chewing as fast as she could. Nat and Felix followed.

They stood uncertainly in the sunshine and walked back the way they had come: Nat, then Felix, then the girls. The bird woman resumed her note, turning her head, the note climbing higher and higher.

Maddy could hear the singer through the wall. The music school was run by a middle-aged couple out of a storefront converted into a warren of cramped studios: two pianos, recording equipment, guitars, sincere teenagers carrying violins. The couple employed young musicians as teachers. Each little studio brightly sterile, the walls decorated with silkscreened posters for concerts.

Milo and his teacher, a heavy woman in her early twenties with a long blond braid and beautiful dark green tattoos spidering over nearly every visible inch of her body, would stand beaming at each other in the hall when she greeted him, looking like they were engaged in a staring contest, before she bore him off to his lesson in the basement studio, where they put the more boisterous junior pupils, and Maddy, with her phone and the book she wasn't reading, settled on the padded bench near the door.

When Milo first started lessons, Maddy would go to the café across the street, until the day there was a woman at the next table meeting with a social worker to discuss custody of her child and her demands on her ex-husband. It took Maddy a while to realize why there were forms on the table, that these two people were not friends and never would be. The woman was filling out paperwork, hesitating over the questions; she wanted help, but the help she wanted seemed obscure, even to her, so amorphous she couldn't define it. She was unreasonable and aging and she wanted justice and she was unhinged, which Maddy realized at the same time as she figured out that the social worker disliked this woman, though she was trying very hard not to. But the woman was so plaintive, with her long list of wrongs, some real, some imagined or at least dwelt on so obsessively that they had broken loose from reality. She squirmed in the chair, bobbing her head like the woman with her high note and her box of coins, who sang on the corner near that nice café with all the baby clothes.

Maddy was repelled by the way this woman fretted at her leather bag, sipped her coffee, examined her rings, looked around for admiration or pity that no one could give her. She was precarious, clinging barely to a social position by becoming a caricature, cavernously thin, studded with heavy ornaments, talking in directionless eddies about what she wanted, what she needed, what her husband owed her and would not give. When she laughed, it was an abrupt shriek, and the social worker looked down at the half-filled-in forms.

Overhearing (as the social worker got up, put on her coat) that they would meet regularly at this time, Maddy stopped going to the café. She did not want to see the woman again. In her presence, Maddy felt herself sliding away; the woman had seemed so established at first glance, so firmly rooted in her demands and her privilege, and yet it would not save her. She was about to fall away into the dark, and she did not seem to know it. She thought she would be given everything she wanted because she wanted it.

Maddy believed in warnings. The bird woman. The woman in the café. A woman she had seen last week at a streetcar stop weeping into her phone, wailing over and over, *Why are you doing this?* Maddy walked to the next stop but could still hear the woman, the disbelief in her voice that was the disbelief of the woman shouting at the cars about Yugoslavia and the disbelief of the woman in the café who would not be given anything.

She didn't want to guess wrong. She could see herself in a mingy apartment demanding money from Alex, no message on her phone, sitting in a café enumerating her wrongs, twisting her rings on her fingers, the people at other tables hoping not to catch her eye. Sitting in the cheapest bars with her old friends comparing notes on failed auditions, on casting calls for which they were too old, hoping against hope they might get another commercial, working for a catering company, dyeing their hair over the sink. Maddy would still be a universe away from her younger self, protecting her vocal cords from cigarette smoke, reciting Shakespeare in the middle of the night, but no one would envy her anymore. There wouldn't be the flicker of concealed impatience when she complained about not getting the acting job, because there would be no husband in the wings to buy her a lamp made of lacquered paper, to barely notice the credit card bill, there would only be a small basement apartment and heating soup on the stove, tacking up scarves over the windows so she wouldn't see the passing legs of strangers, the old furnace clanking near her single bed.

The woman could be a warning that she must stay married to Alex, half listening across the breakfast table while he answered work emails, Alex attending to what she said the way she attended to Milo's nattering. She was inconsequential to his life, she thought, her lip trembling, he didn't take her seriously, she must take herself seriously before it was too late, it was almost too late, soon she wouldn't be allowed to become who she was meant to be. There was a secret destiny for Maddy's special life, and the woman in the café made her think she might not get it.

So she perched on the bench in the waiting room, and that was when she heard the singer. One of the reasons Maddy insisted that Milo keep coming was so she could hear this woman sing.

She was probably in her sixties and she was learning torch songs. She would arrive early, standing near the bench where Maddy sat, nodding hello absently, already preparing herself. Shaking out her hands, humming under her breath, nothing theatrical in this, she did not want Maddy to admire her focus, would have preferred that Maddy not be there, and Maddy ached, recalling that feeling of creating a spaciousness inside yourself, emptying yourself out. Maddy thought most people were mistaken about performers, believing them self-centred. That was true only of bad performers. Good ones were self-effacing. The woman was not a performer, good or bad, but she knew about letting go of herself.

Maddy watched the woman's face grow calm, her attention fixed on the small vibration in her throat. She wore loud silky clothes and dangling earrings that didn't suit her (she was a grandmotherly white woman with thinning brown hair twisted up and slipping from a brass clasp), and that was part of her courage.

When her teacher came out to find her, she would break into a smile of adoration that was painful to see, but he answered with a smile of his own, and though this was his job, he appeared genuine. He looked barely out of his teens, plump like the woman, a gay Asian kid with big glasses, perhaps this music was his salvation. Such pure love existed between these two, Maddy thought, not for each other but for these songs that no one except musical theatre obsessives and old ladies sang anymore. They had discovered something they found beautiful, and of course the woman paid for the lessons and the young man was most likely horribly in debt for some kind of impractical performance degree, yet this was held between them.

Maddy looked down at her phone. Nothing.

She could hear the lesson, overwhelming the more contained students with their teachers in the other rooms.

It had to be you
It had to be you
I wandered around, and I finally found
The somebody who
Could make me be true
And could make me be blue
And even be glad
Just to be sad – thinking of you

He accompanied her on the piano, singing along to correct her phrasing. Sometimes he played her a recording of whatever song she was learning that day, pausing at points to imitate it, then get her to imitate his imitations, and both of them were almost comically inadequate compared to Billie Holiday and Frank Sinatra and Ella Fitzgerald and whoever else. Neither of them had particularly strong voices. But it didn't matter, Maddy thought, because the woman came every week for a year and every week they greeted each other and sang. The woman did not improve much and never would, but that was not the point, the point was their unstinting useless gladness. Listening, while knowing she did not love her husband and terrified of the woman in the café and all the women like her and with no message on her phone, it was sufficient to know this existed.

Sylvie hoped Clio would give her a sign, but Clio's face was empty. This must be another test. She would have to guess the right moment, but it was closing fast, they were passing by. It was like in a movie where the hero ran through a door as it slid shut, escaping death at the last minute, leaving his coat caught in the door. She would be that heroic and that clever. Her hand stung as she reached out, the flaps of skin pulling apart again. The bird woman's eyes closed for the high note. The sting of metal on Sylvie's open skin.

Looking up from her coins, she turned her head. Someone hovered behind her left shoulder. All day, she didn't know who it was, she couldn't turn fast enough, the man or the woman stepped back whenever she turned, she sang her note, looked over her shoulder, this time she would be faster, no, no, no, no one, she failed, and the smaller girl reached out, she didn't see it but she saw it, she stopped her note, she pointed, screaming, at the guilty girl.

It was all Clio. He knew. Fucking Clio.

He turned in time to see Sylvie bend quickly. The bird woman (he didn't want to call her that, it was Clio's name for her, but he couldn't shake it, she was curved like a hawk, hooked) had looked away. She was searching for something behind her, something she felt brushing her shoulder. He understood that, something brushing close, gone when you looked. Like a wing but not a wing. That feeling that something was surrounding you. Only, for him there was excitement, and for the woman with her coins there was just fear. He needed to defend her because the world for her was a rush of terrible battering wind, or water emptying through a hole. A blind force bearing down on her that she couldn't help. The astonishing pull he felt when the day was about to reveal that what was hidden inside it was for her only horror; for her nothing good was concealed behind surfaces. She was bent over from defending herself. He must defend her.

He knew it was Clio forcing Sylvie. It was always Clio.

His parents thought Clio couldn't help herself, but Clio helped herself all the time.

Sylvie was fast, not fast enough. The woman saw. And he saw everything. He'd been on his guard, ready to see everything. They would have to believe him now.

The woman's scream hit him in his chest like a punch. (Was that what a punch felt like? He didn't know. He wanted to know.) The woman pointed at Sylvie, her finger shook. Sylvie backed away. She hadn't expected this.

This was something happening at last. He looked at Nat, at Sylvie, saw no one would believe the woman, but he had seen. No one was on the woman's side, no one was on his side, not even his mother, though she pretended.

He shouted at Sylvie over the woman screaming. The scream turned inside him, opened him up, like wings exploding from his back, slicing from his shoulder blades. Clio stood in front of Sylvie, who was crying now, he was glad. But if she kept crying, no one would blame her for anything. He pushed Clio out of the way, grabbing at Sylvie's face to get her to stop, she put her hands over her face, he clawed at her hands, Nat pulled him off, and there was blood, why blood?

He ran, yelling back to Nat that he knew what he'd seen. The light turned, horns and slammed brakes and swerving cars, echoing inside Felix like the woman's scream.

Nat called to him. He didn't stop running.

Nat chased him, losing speed as she lost conviction. Stopped at the corner. The girls followed, curiously unhurried, as if Felix's flight put them above suspicion. The woman didn't follow.

She waited for them to catch up. Sylvie's blotched thin face, her freckles appearing darker. Maria or Marianna sat back on the pavement, shouting. Clio whispered in Sylvie's ear. Clio the Final Girl, walking away, detached and witty in her blood-soaked clothes.

'Mama. *Look*.'

Clio offered Sylvie's open palm.

'She didn't do anything.'

Clio pushed Sylvie's hand up to Nat's face as if she had not understood.

'Look. *Look*.'

There was a red line along Sylvie's palm, growing wider. Felix's ragged nails, the rage in his face. She had no idea what she should do or what she had seen (nothing, nothing). The thought of talking to Maddy made her burn and tremble, like Sylvie shaking and crying.

Sylvie had covered her head against Felix as the woman accused her. Felix was so much larger than Sylvie. He'd grabbed Sylvie's wrists as Nat pulled him off, wrenched away from her, and ran, shouting that he'd seen Sylvie stealing, he knew what he'd seen. But Nat had seen nothing.

Nat saw him disappear at the corner. Running, his anger made his body seem older, more coherent, the man's body he would have soon. She was out of breath.

She led the girls across the street. Clio had her arm around Sylvie's shoulders, held her uncut hand. Sylvie, pink and righteous, cried steadily. She wiped her nose on the hem of her shirt, becoming younger as in Nat's mind Felix grew unwieldy, more threatening. By the time they reached the other side, the bird woman had subsided, her shouting lapsing into the noise of the street, disquieting but distant as a faraway siren.

They turned off the larger street, down toward the schoolyard. The girls dawdled, arms linked, Clio's head bent to Sylvie in a parody of adult solicitude. Nat should make Sylvie turn out her pockets, but couldn't imagine forcing her to. Sylvie raised the cut hand to her face, blew along it. The cut seemed to have stopped bleeding.

Nat walked quickly, the traffic fading, a stretch of silence before passing the schoolyard and heading home. She heard the pounding music from the men on the porch before she could see them.

Nat couldn't see Felix. Well, he would walk as he always did when he wasn't lying on his bed upstairs. Walk aimlessly, Sylvie's blood under his nails.

She wanted to trust him. She didn't trust him.

They were at the head of Maddy's street.

The smoking woman was still on the porch. The younger man with the scar was talking; she had the humouring, patient look of a woman who'd listened to a man talk for a long time. The two older men slumped on the front steps, drunk.

She imagined asking: *Have you seen my son?* Describing him as if they didn't know who he was or who she was. A missing-person report, the boy on the milk carton. *Medium build, light brown hair, moves forcefully, knocks things over, last seen wearing a dirty T-shirt and shorts, black Converse with mud on the soles, needs a haircut, needs something to do with his time, needs friends, needs another life.*

The smoking woman would get to her feet, the men come down the steps, they'd go looking, the whole neighbourhood out looking for Felix, calling down alleyways, checking the playground, the schoolyard. He was too old for that. She was on her own. He was.

She couldn't make herself walk down Maddy's street. She must. The young man had run a hose from the excavated house, water running along the sidewalk where it curved at the train tracks.

She saw Maddy coming home, holding Milo's hand. Together they jumped ritually over the stream from the hose, gathering into runnels and finding the sewer. Maddy pulled Milo into the house.

The young man was in the front yard of the ruined house, adding to the pile of garbage. He'd taken his shirt off again. She could just see the tattoo, the lettering she almost recognized. Her grandmother, trying to teach her Russian, giving up.

He'd thrown his shirt onto one of Maddy's planters, it clung to the spindles of dead echinacea (Maddy made her own tinctures). He lit a cigarette.

She turned back to the girls, but they had slipped away. Nat saw the smoking woman hold out her hand to the man with the scar, he pulled her up out of the chair and she went unsteadily down the steps.

Nat wondered what it would be like to sit all day, drinking beer on the porch, talking. She would never know. Those men would never come into her house, she would never be invited to sit with them. She was lonely watching the woman linger at the gate. As if she, Nat, didn't understand simple companionship, too intent on her theories. She wanted someone to offer her a seat on a front porch, a beer. She could weep for her loneliness, how large it was, hidden in plain sight.

Felix, she guessed, would walk until dark.

Did I give him the wrong life? The only person she might have asked was her own mother, who must have looked at Nat a long time ago and realized she wanted nothing her mother was offering, that Nat was planning her escape. But of course she could not say that to her mother, a tetchy woman living alone, who, when they visited, asked the children nothing about their lives. Nat asked her mother nothing. Felix would not ask Nat anything.

She went slowly to Maddy's. The dog was gone from the woman's porch. The wind was picking up, filling the tarps in the empty upper window holes of the house next door like dirty sails. She could see Maddy through the screen door, going into the kitchen, but Milo, who Nat did not trust as far as she could throw, turned in the hall at Nat's tentative knock. His face, usually so animated, neutral as a bare wall. She gestured to him to open the door. He didn't move, as if he thought she couldn't see him.

Sylvie kept crying. Clio moved away from her into the yard, sat on the bench. The cut on Sylvie's hand hurt, dirty from the coins she could feel shifting in her pocket. Muffled by the cloth. Without speaking, they'd agreed, Sylvie thought. She could feel agreement thrumming between them. It was convincing that Felix had cut her hand, she almost forgot the truth herself. And they hadn't actually said, she thought. They hadn't accused him. Nat had just decided to believe them, and it was easy. Felix had hurt her. She was blameless. And she'd proved herself to Clio. Her hand throbbed. They sat.

But Clio's face was wrong, that probing frown.

'Why did you do that?' Clio asked.

Sylvie stopped crying.

'Do what?'

'She was an *unhoused person.*'

'But you wanted me to.'

'I didn't.'

'You said – '

'No I didn't.' She crossed her legs, watched Sylvie experimentally. 'I wouldn't do that. God. Don't worry, I won't tell anyone. I won't get you in trouble.'

'But you – '

'I think you should go home,' Clio said.

Clio was so convincing that Sylvie had no answer, thinking over what Clio had asked, her memory wavering. Maybe Clio hadn't asked her anything. She'd made it up. The coins whispered in her pocket. She stood, dragging her feet through the dust, which billowed in the sun. Turning back at the fence, she saw Clio sitting dreamily on the bench, looking up at the sky, beautiful, alone.

There was a clump of dust under the hall table, shaped like a loosely curled fist. She thought maybe she could reach it. Hide it in her pocket, under the lozenges. Her daughter-in-law came to clean the house sometimes, but she didn't check under tables, she didn't use enough bleach and what she did use she didn't wipe properly. White streaks in the corners.

She could see the clock from where she lay. It was gold and white, plastic painted to look like plaster. She could see the time. No one was coming. She would lie here a little longer. Gabriel wouldn't be home yet. She had time before she heard his key.

In the first lockdown she'd stay awake listening for his key. He took his walks at night then, sometimes till dawn, when he'd meet no one. The click at the door, half curse, the light beginning at the edge of the sky, she'd huddle in the little bedroom beside the bathroom, rigid with fear, listening for the bolt sliding.

She'd never been more afraid of him, thinking the world had disappeared and it would be only the two of them, forever, like when she'd pressed her palms to his glass box at the hospital and known there was something inside him.

With the world gone, the thing inside him was nearer.

Bobby didn't come into the house for almost a year. He left groceries for her on the porch, waved through the screen door, the blue paper mask slipping.

She must stay in the house with Gabriel always. The radio said so, Bobby said so. Gabriel walked up and down the stairs unnecessarily, heavy-footed; she stayed in her bedroom with the radio on.

Sometimes, when she slept fitfully and woke, it wasn't the door opening that woke her. Her eyes would spring open in the half-dark of the smaller bedroom she'd moved to when her husband died. She feared the dark, kept a nightlight on by her dresser. Bobby had given her a nightlight of the Virgin Mary, but she hated it, hid it in a drawer, which was fine now that Bobby would never come inside again. She had a smooth pink nightlight, like a doll's plastic flesh lit up. What was that sound? Not the lock, not the door. A growling, a gnawing. Gabriel slept in the big bedroom overlooking the street, he'd taken the curtains off the windows, he didn't mind the alien light from the street lamp shining over him. When their father died, Gabriel and Bobby took apart her old bed and Bobby threw it away (he said he hadn't, but what else would he do with it?). Gabriel moved in his single bed, the scratched blue pressboard frame of his childhood, and his posters of wolves.

That was the growling, she thought. Gabriel was gnawing a carcass, crouched in the far corner of his room, half-hidden by the bed. She'd dreamed it, but it didn't help to tell herself that, she knew she wasn't dreaming, sitting up to remind herself of the verses on the wall. *(You prepare a table before me in the presence of mine enemies.)* Gabriel was a wolf with a wolf's habits. If she got up and walked down the hall in her bare feet, the linoleum cold under her, pushed open the door, he would startle, snarling, his eyes catching the light greenly. His eyes were wrong. She couldn't go and look at him. It was a dream, and if she went into his room it might not be. She must not see him naked, chewing quickly. He'd gone down into the basement hunting rats.

After the first month there was a new smell. Gabriel was hiding bones under his bed.

The lockdown ended, the smell went away. He must have buried the bones in the backyard. She tried to put it out of her mind. He left during the days again, Bobby came again, and Emily and her mother with their closed-mouth smiles.

She watched the street again and saw the people walking around, greeting each other as if nothing had happened. There was no one to tell about the smell. She'd imagined it, sealed inside with Gabriel, wondering how long until he ate her. She would be bones under his bed.

Water from the tap, running white and frothy, cooling, standing for a moment in the glass. Water over her face like when she was a child, working the pump in the yard, the bucket overflowing, darkening between the stones. The different sun, the different sky, the sand on the shore. Dried crabs scattering in the high wind. She was so thirsty.

She could reach slowly. She gathered up the soft ball of dust and hid it in her pocket.

She'd go home and feed him now. The pavement tipped a bit, but she'd been worse, she'd seen worse. Gabe drank two for every one she did, and he'd gotten himself home or wherever. The metal gate was warm from all that sun. People would be complaining about the heat soon, but not her. Bring it on. She had her fans and her porch, she could take it. The late nights in summer when you didn't bother going to bed, what was the point, you sat all night looking out at the street, that's when she noticed stars and the low swoop of bats. She loved that time. The middle of the night, alone except for him beside her, thumping his tail to let her know he was there.

Clio, on the bench, tipped back her chin as far as she could, letting the sun onto her throat, thinking of herself lying on a beach. There was a picture in the dentist's office of a woman lying on a beach. It was black and white, the camera pulled in close so you could see beads of water on the woman's skin, how the cloudy grey sand clung to her forearm, flung over the edge of the striped towel. Her face was turned away, just a loose knot of dark hair slumped to one side, the strands wandering over her ear. The tendons stretched in her neck, like she was ready to spring up. Clio was going to be like that woman. Lying on the towel, her skin gleaming like meat. Resting but ready to leave any time she wanted.

She liked looking at the woman on the beach to distract herself from her terror of the dentist. They thought she was afraid of the pain, but Clio didn't mind needles, numbness flooding her mouth, the dull tug of pliers. It interested her, to think carefully, *This is pain*, as the needle slid into the gum. She was afraid the dentist would tell her she needed braces. Nat always said she would probably need braces, looking critically at her teeth, and reminded Clio how lucky she was, pointing at her own crooked incisors, saying as if for the first time that her mother couldn't afford to get her children braces. Clio would be condemned to a mouthful of wet dark metal, elastics and trapped chewed food, to smiling with her lips pressed closed. And it took years. Just when she'd gotten this shirt and her gold butterflies. Noah, who sat next to her, finally looking at her. He wouldn't anymore.

How far back could her head go? She wanted the sun to reach. The tilt also made her think of horror movies, the surprising expanse of neck, a throat slit clean. Ear to ear. She liked watching that moment. When what was inside spilled out, blood in fountains, flowing like the champagne tower at her cousin's wedding. Something so drastic it could never be repaired. No one would attempt to make it right. It was finished.

The young woman on the beach towel was who Clio would become if she could just be patient. She didn't know if she could muster enough patience. When she listened to that song with Sylvie, over and over, about coming home again and wishing you were still a child, she couldn't wait to be old enough to wish for that. To be so far away from her home and her family and her friends that thinking of them made her ache, but with a crisp adult authority that would not dwell on sadness. She would have too much to do; she couldn't linger. She didn't know what the much was, but something important she hadn't thought of yet.

Nat and Frankie, talking while they made dinner, gossiping about people they knew, or had known, before children, people they rarely saw. Listening from the other room, doing her homework at the dining room table because they insisted she should be near them. Felix refused to. So she sat with her legs curled around the crosspiece of the new chair (they needed a new set of chairs, along with the new floor and walls), listening. *I mean, you have to remember she left home at sixteen.* She didn't know who had left. Or why you had to remember. Just that it was possible. If someone could go, she could. Not dramatically, not in anger. Just because it was time. She pictured herself explaining to Nat and Frankie, standing in the doorway of their room, tall and thin in strappy heels and a silky blue shift dress, like the dress she'd seen the woman wearing at the restaurant they'd taken her to on her birthday. Clio would explain it was time for her to go and they would understand, they would be saddened, but she was old enough. She'd appear in the doorway of their room and they'd sit up in bed, formal and proud, like in a movie she'd seen where a girl crept into her parents' room to tell them exciting news, only the girl cried and Clio wouldn't. Nat thought Felix would never get out of his bed; perhaps she would be pleased that Clio, grown so tall and pretty, was capable of leaving.

She pictured herself coming to visit, when she lived in another city, another country, wheeling a small suitcase, her hair, sharply cut and shining, brushing her shoulders. Her parents said she didn't understand consequences, but she did. She wanted to make a life in which she was free of consequences. That wasn't the same as not understanding they existed.

The girl at school, the mean drawings they'd made. It was just a joke. She'd led Sylvie into it, but Sylvie begged to be led, she expected it, Clio shouldered the weight of all of Sylvie's love, and it was so heavy. The coins tarnished, slumped in the cardboard box. She wanted to be alone on the beach, the sand clinging to her smooth skin (she checked every morning in the mirror for blemishes, frowning clinically at her pores). Sylvie needed her to be ruthless and then was destroyed when she was as Sylvie expected. She wouldn't let Sylvie blame her. Not inside herself.

She pictured going to Sylvie's house, taking the coins, walking back along the street to the café. The woman still there. Clio would wait until she wasn't looking and return them, letting them glimmer through her open fingers. Gone before anyone saw her. Slipping back the way she came, the butterflies sparkling in her lobes. So graceful, so alone. Making it finished.

The sun was warm on her throat. She could almost feel the sand underneath her, stretching away, the waves slowly curling toward the pale soles of her perfect feet.

In Maddy's kitchen, the surface of the tart appeared grey, the ridges she'd sculpted ragged like broken plaster. The berries had bled together, red blots spreading beneath each shiny bead. She should have planned to bring the berries with her; she saw herself cutting berries on Nat's new counter, on one of Nat's inlaid cutting boards, her fingers stained, pausing to sip wine. If only she'd thought ahead.

She'd made herself leave her phone in her pocket when she'd hung up her jacket.

There would be no message. There would be nothing ever again. The tart was dingy, the crust not as perfect as she'd thought. Some of the berries turning syrupy, slumped as if pressed down by a finger. Milo called to her from the hall.

Nat stood on the doorstep and Maddy leaned against the open screen door, Milo behind her, watching. She felt his hair. Stickiness from the jam on his hands that morning, a gritty strand. Tonight she would wash it.

'Are the girls here?'

'I don't think so. I just got home.'

As if on cue, they heard the back door. There was Sylvie, pretending to be in a hurry. Seeing Nat, she paused at the foot of the stairs, thinking. It looked to Maddy like she was avoiding the light, her skin greyed like the tart on the kitchen table. Deciding, she ran upstairs.

Maddy laughed. 'They never want to talk anymore, do they? I'm glad I've got this one!'

She tugged gently at Milo's hair, and he leapt back out of reach, curled himself up on the bottom stair with his cape wrapped around himself.

Nat's mouth was dutifully set.

Maddy let her own smile fade. 'Is everything okay?'

'Sylvie cut her hand.'

'Oh. She seems fine?'

'It was Felix.'

Maddy wanted to dash up the stairs and demand to see Sylvie's hand, imagined Sylvie hiding her hand under her shirt. She sensed Sylvie not in her room, just out of sight at the top of the stairs. She stepped out, closing the screen door. The young man was smoking in the front yard again. His back was to them, he was looking at his phone, but Maddy thought his shoulders lifted, a new awareness of her presence.

'It was Felix?'

Nat told her about the woman, the coins, his torn nails, the cut on Sylvie's hand, Felix running, yelling over his shoulder. That she didn't know where Felix was. 'He said he saw her stealing.'

Maddy couldn't decide how to proceed. There was wounded Sylvie upstairs, and Felix with his paranoid resentments that Nat sometimes confided in her about (but she couldn't bring that up, it would end future confessions, and she wanted those, surprised out of Nat by accident). Felix must be in the wrong.

She could run upstairs and bandage Sylvie's hand, leaving Nat standing at a loss outside. The main point was that Sylvie was hurt and Sylvie wouldn't do something like that, and even if she had, it was just a childish thing, the heap of coins, beyond Sylvie's comprehension. Nat shouldn't be so grim about what everything meant. But Maddy couldn't think of what to say.

Milo came to the screen door, watching, twisting the fabric of his cape in his hands, and as Nat hesitated in her accusation, wanting Maddy to – what? – accuse her own child so Nat's son was not to blame, Maddy let herself dislike Nat, the way Alex did, finding her self-righteous. Maddy didn't want to be like Alex. There was nothing wrong with Alex, but she wouldn't share his opinions.

Opinions.

Bed.

Dinner table.

Household.

Children.

Life.

Stop it. Nothing was wrong except that she had never loved him. But she wouldn't be the woman in the café, she wouldn't unhook the paper lamp. She would not be to blame.

Nat, in front of her, not talking.

'I think I should go look at Sylvie's hand,' Maddy said, her tone light, as if this whole incident was a joke.

Nat would not be light. 'I think you need to talk to her. I'll talk to Clio too, of course. If they stole from the woman, there have to be consequences.'

'Yes. Of course.'

'He's sure he saw it,' Nat added lamely.

'Did *you* see it?'

'No.' She sounded miserable.

Maddy kept quiet: a trick from one of her old acting exercises. Keep quiet long enough, and the other person, unable to bear it, will have to commit themselves in some way. Maddy could keep quiet the longest.

Milo's face was against the glass, the tip of his nose squashed white.

'I can talk to Felix,' Nat said. 'I mean, I will when I find him. But he's sure he saw it.'

'Yes. You said. I should check on Sylvie.'

'He gets so angry, he didn't mean to hurt her.' Nat reddened, hearing herself.

'I don't think it matters whether he *meant to*. I'll talk to Sylvie when she feels better, but she's very vulnerable these days, you know. I'm going to wait till she's ready. It's not going to make a difference if he meant to. Even if she did anything, it wasn't serious. He could really hurt someone. He's going to hurt someone.'

Nat had no answer.

'So maybe you should talk to Felix before anything else happens. Excuse me, I want to go find Sylvie.'

'You're right. I'm sorry. You're right.'

Maddy didn't move, amazed by her victory. Nat looked ready to weep, without guile or plan. Red as a stain flooding a white skirt.

'I'm sorry. I should go find Felix.'

She moved away, trudging along the street toward her own house. Maddy, reckless with her gains, pursued her down the sidewalk.

'What? I'm going. I'll talk to him.'

'Do you still want us to come tonight? Should we still come?'

Nat looked bemused, and it was Maddy's turn to blush.

'Do you not want to come anymore?'

'No. No. Of course I want to come – '

'Okay. Good. Okay.'

She kept walking. Maddy twisted the hem of her shirt in her hands like Milo twisting his cape, watching her go. She felt she must sit on the sidewalk and keen, and wanted to run after Nat, who in Maddy's mind had the upper hand again, but if she ran after Nat, she'd say she didn't blame Felix, she didn't blame the girls, she wanted no one to be to blame. No one was to blame, not even Alex. It was just that everyone was mistaken.

It was too late now, Nat was gone, looking for Felix, Sylvie was upstairs with her hand bleeding, Milo was watching her through the screen door. She went inside, calling Sylvie's name, and he slipped past her down the steps.

God, these women, Ilya thought, they didn't fight, they didn't know how to fight. They behaved as if a fight was the worst thing. Like everything would break apart between them if they showed they were angry. They believed they were important enough for that. He thought of his mother, her shrill feuding, her grumbling along the hallway of her apartment building, past the doors of people she had stopped speaking to, or people she would shout at in the laundry room, shaken with her own fury and uprightness. In a few months, those friendships would be repaired, sometimes by anger at a third person. His mother was not bearable, but at least she understood it was not so easy to be broken, that her life was not some kind of filigreed thing she had to shelter in her hands.

Did they notice he was listening? They were both nervous of him, though the other one didn't interest him, not only because she was too old, part of her nervousness was thinking he cared about her, that she somehow offended him. He didn't care how anyone lived as long as they knew that their life was not delicate. That they would disappear like everyone else, without any real disruption to the world. How to make them know? But it wasn't his job. Was it? The sun was slipping lower, touching the houses. He should go home.

He retrieved his shirt from the dead plant, wiped his hands on it. As he looked down, the shirt did not seem to be clothing anymore. A rag he'd picked up by mistake, garbage belonging to someone else. He panicked briefly. Everything belonged to someone else. What if this feeling kept growing, a fungal creep, not just the shirt, the hands holding it, not his?

Committing, he wiped his face on the shirt, dried the sweat from his neck. Rubbed it over himself like a towel. His hands were his. He rubbed hard at his scalp, almost bruising. The tender skin beneath the stubble of hair was his. He closed his eyes, wiped his face again. The skin of his eyelids was his. Gold and red behind his eyes. The lids thin as the skin of an egg, picking at an egg in the morning, peeling away the membrane, looking through it, his mother making him eat eggs, the eggs making him gag. That was his memory. He wasn't lost.

He thought he could hear the other woman calling her son's name. *Felix, Felix*. The son was lost.

He balled the shirt up at the top of his bag, then took it out and threw it on the pile of trash.

No one else had come, and the work on the basement needed at least two people. The front wall loose under his hands, the old mortar coming off on his fingers. The basement a wreck of lapping water, muddied earth, broken concrete heaped in the corners. He didn't want to think about the basement today; he avoided looking into it through the open hole. He should go home.

'Felix! Felix!' came at him again from far away, the alleyway that ran from the cross street where this street ended. He could just see the woman walking, calling, disappearing.

He tried to picture Felix and came up with a stocky boy loping along the sidewalk. Maybe also trying to figure out how to bear his life, because he wasn't a woman so he didn't make the mistake of thinking he was precious (women, weeping over their lives). The boy would know already how easily he could disappear. Ilya remembered Felix stopping to pet the dog on the porch. The dog wasn't on the porch. The old woman must have taken him inside.

Why did no one come all day, what did they know that he didn't? What if they'd walked off the job, what if no one was being paid anymore and he was the only person stupid enough to show up? They didn't tell him. Simon would have told him.

He needed the money. The lawyer talked about lawsuits, about settlements. Ilya didn't want to plan on settlements, like his father imagining his future wealth with no actual expectation of anything beyond disability payments, if he could even get those. The lawyer promised enough for houses, but Ilya knew better than to believe him. Ilya would not be deceived into hoping for anything. He wouldn't be tricked by promises of houses, as the wives were, mourning their husbands but letting themselves imagine pale blue carpets and fenced backyards, strong coffee served with cake for guests who would be respectful in their envy, mindful of loss, but visibly covetous, blinded by the flash of tile in the kitchen.

If the owner was finally broke, someone should have told Ilya. He didn't know how to talk to the other men, or not enough, or he didn't joke enough, maybe that was it. He couldn't figure out what was funny, why. He didn't join in when they called the red-haired woman a bitch, and he could have said she was a bitch, she was sometimes, but he loved her sadness. All he needed to do was copy what the other men did: putting out their cigarettes on her side of the property line, gesturing obscenities as she shut the door, timed so she didn't see and couldn't not see either. Ilya was a good guy. He wanted her to know that. Why hadn't he spoken to her earlier? Sometimes he thought about telling her he knew she was unhappy. Formally, as if her unhappiness were an official matter, the way the lawyer told the wives their grief was something official, something with result. He would stand very close to her, telling her that he knew, and she wouldn't move away. She would stay near him.

He finished packing his tools, locked the door pointlessly since anyone could have come in through the ragged hole in front of the threshold, though you couldn't climb to the first floor from the basement without a ladder, and he'd lifted it away. He adjusted the cover with his boot. It should be steel, not plywood. It was too easy to shift. The hole was too deep for that flimsy sheet. He could drive his boot through it if he kicked hard enough. Was that the rats returning now that there was no other sound?

The music from the men on the porch had stopped.

He could hear the water, down in the dark.

There was the small boy in his red cape. He didn't know yet how easily he could disappear. Ilya liked the other boy better.

'What's that?' He pointed at Ilya's neck.

Ilya clapped his hand to his neck as if the boy had seen something clinging there.

'No, the tattoo.'

'It's a dragon. You know what a dragon is?'

'I know what a dragon is. What does it say?'

'What does a *dragon* say? A dragon roars!'

The boy regarded him impassively, his arms crossed over his chest. 'I mean the *words*, dumbass.'

Ilya smiled indulgently. That would show him. The boy looked disappointed. 'It's a proverb.'

'What's a proverb?'

'Don't you know what a proverb is?'

'Something that isn't English?'

'No, dumbass. A proverb is like ... A bird in the hand. Have your cake and eat it too. Look before you leap. The grass is always greener. An enemy will agree but a friend will argue.'

'I don't know any of those. What's the one on your neck mean?'

Ilya pretended to cover the writing running alongside the dragon's head. 'I can't tell you. It's a secret.'

'I want to know.' He kicked at the board with one bare foot.

'Don't you dare touch that,' Ilya said.

'I *know* not to touch it,' the boy said, startled.

'You could fall in. You could drown,' Ilya insisted, as if the boy had not spoken. It wasn't accurate either, a few inches of water down there at most, it would be hard to imagine the boy drowning unless he fell in headfirst and knocked himself out. But Ilya wanted the boy to be afraid. It made him feel benevolent and important to make the boy afraid. And he wanted to keep talking to him. The boy would pay attention. Someone would pay attention to Ilya.

'There are rats down there.'

'I know,' the boy said again.

'So many, many rats,' Ilya said softly.

The boy stepped back. 'How many?'

'A thousand.'

The boy's eyes widened as he pictured rats marshalling below the house. Lashing tails, squeals. Red-eyed like old-movie villains, so much better than the few unconcerned creatures waddling out of their holes. 'What will they do?'

'Rats? Do how?'

'What would they do to *me*?' the boy asked daringly, looking at Ilya's face.

Ilya thought it had been a long time since anyone had looked him full in the face. He crouched, spoke into the soft whorl of the boy's ear. 'They would *eat* you!'

The boy leapt back, delighted with his own terror, and Ilya laughed, and the boy joined in shrilly, relieved. 'No way,' he said approvingly, shaking his head. 'No way. I don't believe you.'

To prolong the game, Ilya leaned down again, speaking into the opposite ear. 'I never lie. Don't touch the board.'

Standing, he let his hand rest on the boy's head, and the boy stood ceremonially straight. Ilya took his hand away quickly, taken aback at himself, shocked by the feel of the boy's hair, his attention, his cunning.

The boy was planning something. Ilya must leave fast and not see it. He went to his truck, glancing at the pleated curtains of the old woman's house, which didn't move. She must not be at her window after all.

He rounded the corner, driving slowly, watching for children and dogs and blundering old women, mindful of the dipping sun in his eyes, of the swing of the red cape as the boy bent down, but Ilya turned safely and was gone.

Evening

The light comes back. It is a later light, slanted, appearing from the hole. First a dragging sound, then a drift of dust falling in the brightened air. The pump works mightily. A rectangle of light appears, grows.

The rats retreat to a ledge of the back wall, watching. This wall is the strongest, which they feel in the vibrations underneath them when the house above shakes. The front wall jitters, clots of earth and mortar falling into the water.

The pump works. The water churns. The rats sniff the water. The walls swell.

Above, an arm appears, waving, reaching. Handfuls of sawdust and earth thrown into the water. Then a head, trying to see inside.

The rats go into their tunnels, stay near the entrances, waiting to see what will happen.

The head streams with light, the face shadowed. The head turns, teeth gleaming. Disappears, and then the arm again waving, trying to touch the streaming front wall. Finding it, the hand closes around a chunk of masonry, pries it loose, throws it. The arm withdraws and reappears, withdraws and reappears, flinging things from the heap of garbage piled in front of the house. Down come a few plastic bags, a coil of wire, a branch, a length of safety chain. The chain, a lucky hit, falls near the pump, entangles it. A few moments of stand-off, the pump straining, growling, the chain pulled further and further in.

Stutter and sparks and a delicate plume of brownish smoke, and the pump shudders and stops.

The ripples break against the walls, refracted back, slowly diminishing.

In the silence, the rats wait.

The arm waits, the hand waits, fingers outspread in shocked triumph, then pulls back. The head appears at the hole again, trying to see but blocking too much of the light for more than a glimmering impression of the black broken pump. A smell of burnt plastic and hot metal.

The silence is not as total as either the rats or the boy think it is, only marked in contrast with the labour of the pump. Another sound emerges: the water, rising slowly.

The smoke clears. The water is greenish grey.

The head pulls back through the opening, and the rats hear a scramble of feet backing away, see the boy's shadow as he looks over his shoulder to make sure he is not observed. One last thing, a piece of jagged metal from an old vent, is thrown or accidentally kicked into the hole, racketing down the wall, borne up on the water like a raft before it drifts down. The rats hear footsteps retreating. The light flows in undisturbed over the rising water.

His frenzy over, Milo stood in the yard, looking down into the exposed hole, the board shoved away to one side. He could smell smoke. The silence overwhelmed him. He'd broken the pump. This was more than he meant, not what he wanted. He didn't know what he'd wanted. For something to happen, because the day was long and his mother left him alone and tried to make him practise piano and he'd had a vision of flinging things into the interesting dark, as strong as his imaginings of the winning touchdown, of singing to a stadium full of rapt people, of making enough paper snowflakes to cover every window of his house. Beauty. Beauty that was his doing and belonged to him.

The silence was too loud. He was streaked with dust.

No one had seen him. If he went inside now, no one would know it was him. Not like when he wrote his name in black marker along the baseboard, which he couldn't deny though he didn't understand the problem, it was his room, he could mark his room for himself. He brushed at the front of his shirt. He knew if he got inside the house and ran upstairs fast enough, nothing would be his fault. Hiding what he'd done, he would get free of it. Maybe never think of it again. By the time he'd finished washing his hands, he'd be able to convince himself he'd done nothing wrong, and with determination he'd bring himself to believe he'd done nothing at all. The important thing was not to tell anyone. If you didn't tell a secret, it wasn't real.

Sylvie took the box from underneath the bed. The Converse logo showed under the shells, and dried petals stuck on with pliant gobs of white glue. *Clio and Sylvie Forever* sharpied unevenly on the cover.

Too pretty and her mother would not be able to resist opening it, picturing scented keepsakes, girlishness. But if the box was left undecorated, she might throw it away. Sylvie would find it on the dining room table, bound for the trash, and she wasn't allowed to question this; she didn't try. Her mother rampaged intermittently through the house, smiling anxiously, conquering for the moment but knowing she was losing in the long run. Sylvie didn't care what the loss was, she just wanted the storm to die down so she could go about her business.

Clio said they had to keep it at Sylvie's house. Nat looked hard at things, into things, more often and more thoroughly than Maddy. Boxes, drawers, search histories.

That shy knock.

'Sylvie?'

'Yeah?'

'Can you open the door?'

'No thanks.'

'Nat told me what happened. I'm so sorry. Can you open the door please?'

'No.'

'Sylvie. Sweetie.'

'Is Dad home yet?' She didn't want to see him especially, but the effect on Maddy was helpful.

A hurt pause, the possibility of retreat. 'No, darling. Not yet.'

'Oh.'

'Please open the door, I want to look at your hand.'

'It's nothing. It doesn't hurt.'

Hovering, perhaps a step away from the door now. Sylvie just had to get her to keep going.

'Are you sure?'

'Yeah. Don't worry. I'll come down soon.'

Silence.

'Sweetie?'

'Yeah?'

'Is it okay if we still go to Clio's house for dinner?'

Maddy didn't care really, Sylvie thought. She just didn't want to cancel the plan. It wasn't that she was worried about Sylvie. She didn't think about her.

'Sylvie?'

Maybe she could make it up to Clio. She would make Clio remember. 'It's fine.'

Held breath on both sides of the door. Then Maddy moved away.

Steps on the stairs, a pause halfway as if she might come back. She didn't.

Sylvie could hear her talking to Milo in the kitchen, Milo answering in the voice he used when he was guilty. Maddy would not guess or suspect. She would not suspect Sylvie. Clio sighed at Sylvie's luck, Nat lecturing Clio on every slip, imagining she did not.

Sylvie tried to experimentally think of her mother as Maddy. When Clio called her own parents by their names, Sylvie admired her casual tone, like these were people she knew distantly and would soon shake free of. Sylvie was endlessly embarrassed by her mother's violent appreciation of beauty or kindness. Sylvie wanted to be like Clio, coolly skeptical, unassociated.

Sylvie shuffled the coins in her hand, wondering if Clio was done with her at last, and how she would bear it if that were true. She lifted her other hand to her face, bringing it close; the cut across her palm grew wider, gaping pink, until it unfocused. Like the cut and what the day had turned into didn't belong to her, the way Clio was able to act as if nothing was her fault.

Sylvie heard music, not the music on the porch but different music, a brass band, playing one street over or in the schoolyard. Maddy had said something about it, a community band, practice in the afternoons or some evenings, and did Sylvie want to go, did Clio want to. They didn't.

A tuba groaned. Sylvie thought the sound was getting nearer. She wondered whether the girl from school who was afraid of them was there, with her cringing face. Just then the cacophony seemed to settle, come together as a song, but a moment later the men on the porch turned on their music again and outside was just noise.

She opened the box. The fat sky-blue wallet with the brass zipper, stripped of cash. They'd kept the cards, useless now. It was a year old. They'd taken it from a purse left on the bench in the schoolyard. They had not recognized the picture of the woman, who was older, with a puffed pale face like a mushroom and long peacock-green bead earrings brushing her shoulders. Driver's licence, health card, three different credit cards, the bank card with the plastic casing frayed at the edges, gummy with use, a few coffee cards, receipts. Clio was interested only in the cash, which they'd spent over months so no one would suspect. Sylvie didn't want to throw the wallet away. She liked to search for the woman, hoping she would pass her on the street. She would look the woman right in the face and the woman would be confused and smile, no idea who Sylvie was, and Sylvie would know what the woman looked like when she smiled.

Packages of stickers from the stationery store across the bridge, glossy pink plastic eggs with toys inside from the corner store, plastic pearls from a kiosk in the mall, a set of car keys they'd found in the snow, a bracelet from the cringing girl's desk, tiny tarnished links and lumpy charms, most dangerously a necklace, unhooked from the backing, dangling near the lower edge of the long velvet-covered board cluttered with silver. Clio distracted Maddy and the seller at the craft show while Sylvie, nimble-fingered, slid the necklace into the front pocket of her jacket. An amber egg twisted in silver wire.

Sylvie would take the necklace with her when she left home. It evoked a middle-aged woman given to trailing scarves that hid the droop beginning around her throat. Sylvie would wear it anyway, in penance for who she had been, but no one would notice it, except her mother saying, *That's pretty, sweetheart, where is it from?* Sylvie said she didn't know, and went on packing boxes.

Sylvie's memory: the quick work of her fingers, the chain looping into her pocket, the electric sympathy with Clio, the plan that happened without words, knowing when Clio would begin her guileless chatter, cuing Sylvie to drop to her knees, sensing no one was looking. Sylvie hot as metal, brilliantly invisible. About to leave home and begin her real life, she wanted to remember that it was possible to burn like that. To be in thrall to another person. Sylvie wanted that as her destiny, her purpose, and that's what will happen. Pining for other people will take up most of her time. She will have some regrets. But not only. She thinks women who believe in their own autonomy are missing out on an amazing possibility for meaning. Abjection and debasement are inevitable, so why not be honest about it.

She will not mind her mother thinking the necklace was pretty. Her mother will not know what it meant.

The coins warmed, sticky in her hand. She hadn't taken very many. The woman would not have noticed, counting them later, if she counted them. She probably poured them into a jar, an empty plastic ice-cream tub. It was Felix's fault that the woman noticed Sylvie bending down. Her hand hurt where he'd yanked at her; she could almost believe he'd inflicted the cut. Later, when that night supplants what happened in the afternoon, she sometimes forgets the schoolyard, the glass. It's all minor details.

Sylvie brought the coins to her face, inhaled: warm dirty silver, smelling like pavement just before rain. *Petrichor*. She'd learned the word recently, she knew it wasn't exactly the smell of metal, but close. Liking the punch of the word, she repeated it to herself, *Petrichor petrichor*. It made her think of walking with Clio, waiting for the rain to come.

She trailed the coins slowly into the box. Clio had whispered to her as they went into the café that it would be easy to take them, and Sylvie would give Clio what she wanted. She would show Clio her swiftness, her lightness.

She'd been wrong. It was Sylvie's mistake, and everything that happened after – the shouting, Felix grabbing her wrists, Nat talking to her mother on the front steps, her mother tapping at her door – was Sylvie's fault. Sylvie would need to think of a way to apologize to Clio.

Later, as a young woman, she will visit a therapist after having her heart broken by a man she'd hoped to marry. She tries to explain, to describe, the effect of needing to endlessly apologize to Clio (whom she no longer knows), but the therapist isn't interested, the therapist nudges her gently toward her parents, individually and in their marriage, toward the obvious things, and Sylvie understands that's the job but thinks secretly that the therapist is either a bit stupid or too far from childhood to recall or at least be able to imagine that Clio, the force of Clio, might be as important as anything else, might be part of why Sylvie humiliated herself, begging until the man got bored and left. The therapist says Sylvie is deflecting from the main story, and Sylvie remembers Clio throwing pebbles in the air in the schoolyard, Clio telling her to go and leaning her head back on the bench in the afternoon sun. Sylvie smiles suitably. Soon she will meet someone else, who she does marry, though not permanently.

She picked up the coins again, flipping a quarter, watching it turn in the air, not sure what she was betting on, but there was a bet, heads or tails, win or lose. She had lost.

Her stomach was hollow, the pulse in her throat beating hard. Clio knew Sylvie had lost. Clio was the test-setter, the arbiter of winning and losing. Sylvie could only guess.

She was usually good at guessing. Climb the roof of the shed, stretch out the wad of soft tooth-marked pink gum into the hair of the woman beside them on the subway just before their stop, Sylvie's father didn't notice, even though she was right beside him; he was trying to answer an email on his phone. Spit in the drinks at the party, Clio working her tongue, trailing clear bubbles into the ice cubes bobbing in the lemonade. Leave the drawings in the cringing girl's desk. The day they'd both fallen at the same time in the yard, sucked the blood from each other's knees. Copper-salty, mixed with gravel and dirt.

Milo was singing downstairs.

Last year they'd given a concert, taking a laptop into the room behind the kitchen where Maddy had arranged craft supplies in labelled pale blue boxes on white shelves, set up a card table and a sewing machine and the plug-in keyboard that Milo used for piano practice. The bamboo mats grew stained with paint and glue, littered with pins, and Maddy said she preferred it that way, she wanted the house to feel lived-in, but Sylvie remembered her mother's face when she showed them the room she'd made for them, the smooth mats with their green-stitched edges and the folded fabric, pale colours that Sylvie thought matched the boxes, and the notched round metal containers of glitter and cotton balls, each with its own label (Maddy had beautiful handwriting). Sylvie knew she wanted the room to stay like that, waiting and empty. The stains pained Maddy, the way the ribbons were snarled, the wool tangled, the different beads mixed hopelessly together. Sylvie liked the sharpness of the glass beads under her fingers. She opened the vials into a bowl, stirred them, put them back. Her mother would assume Milo had done it; the room was for Milo anyway, Sylvie was too old.

She was too old for the concert, but Milo begged and Maddy made the face that meant Sylvie must be obliging. So they took the laptop into the backroom and balanced it on a stool during dinner and practised duets in front of lyric videos, and the guests stood akimbo, leaning back against the shelves and then straightening up because the containers dug into their spines. She wavered beside the laptop, a little behind Milo, her hand on the space bar, ready to play. The adults distantly humouring, her mother watching Milo, who sang.

Sylvie tried to join him, but her voice dried out, looking at the faces, her mother's face, her mother watching Milo, who raised his arms and lifted his chin, seeming to know exactly where the light was, not like a singer, like an invasive and pitiless plant finding the light, and Sylvie stared at the ground while Milo sang, and it wasn't that Maddy looked at Milo, Sylvie wouldn't mind that so much, he demanded that, he always had, it was that Maddy was sorry for her and that Sylvie could feel something opening underneath her, the ground heaving, like that was adulthood. People feeling sorry for you, forever.

She shoved the box under the bed. The coins whispered and shifted as the box hit the wall.

He was gone, the fucker.

She shouldn't have had the beers, she should have got the new rope. But they wanted her to stay, no one ever wanted her to stay anymore, and then she needed to get home and lie down. He was gone. She was too late.

Noise in her ears, noise coming from the schoolyard, she could almost see that far, flashes of brass on the other side of the chain-link fence, a drum, she could hear it under the music coming from the speakers. The drum pounded in the gaps. What the fuck were they doing, those people marching around the schoolyard? Maybe they'd seen her dog?

She kicked at her step where the wood was rotted and felt it give. She kicked again, wanting her foot to break through.

The girls staring at her dog in the morning, thinking they could stare at her like she didn't stare back, but she saw them, knew they were like dolls in a horror movie, twittering and bloody, with plastic blue eyes rolling back. If they did anything to her dog, she'd make their eyes pop out, blue-and-white plastic eyes bouncing on the pavement. Those girls whispered like their mothers, but at least they didn't pretend.

The mothers didn't stare; they pushed their children's hands toward her dog's head, but with the same rolling eyes. The one with the short hair always on her high horse, saying *my partner* or *my wife,* like anyone gave a shit. She'd been around the block a few times herself, back in the day, not that that was anybody's business. No one cared.

Sitting down on the top step, she lit a cigarette.

She saw the boy again, poor kid in his dirty shirt, scraping his feet along the pavement, kicking a stone, kicking at her fence.

'Hey! Hey!'

He stopped. 'Sorry.'

'My dog's gone.'

'Can I help you find him?'

She liked him. She could remember being that angry, not knowing why. He didn't know you grow out of it, sort of. Hair falling over his forehead, his nails ripped, packed with grime, he wiped his hands down the front of his shirt. He looked like he was covered with sand, blinking sand out of his eyes.

'Did your sister and her friend cut the rope?'

Looking down at it, she considered. It looked chewed, not cut. But she wanted someone to blame. He did too. He thought, nodded slowly. 'I bet they did.'

She got to her feet. 'Well, your sister's not your fault.'

'My sister's a *bitch*.'

She came down the stairs and hit the back of his head, pleased. 'Wash out your mouth.'

'Sorry.' He was pleased too.

He looked like nobody was on his side, she knew about that. She could just say, *Yeah, those girls are real bitches*, but she stopped herself. Save it. 'His name's Ringo. He doesn't see that good anymore. You need to come up to him slow. Don't be loud. He's scared.'

'Why's he scared?'

'He's a rescue. The first owner used to kick the shit out of him. He's a good dog, but he's scared of everything. You have to be really gentle with him.'

'Why did he leave?'

'I guess spring got into him.'

The boy wanted so much to be helpful, looking around the corner of her house to prove himself, like the dog was right there. Good thing she'd never had kids, it was too much already, how he wanted to be needed. Dodged a bullet on that one, she thought.

'Okay. I'll go this way, you go down that way.'

'What should I do if I see him?'

'Get in close and call, kneel down so you don't look too tall. He gets scared of men.'

He dipped his head.

'Men, boys, whatever. You're tall enough.'

He flushed, and she knew enough not to show she noticed.

'Hats too, he's scared of men in hats. I bet that asshole who had him before used to wear a hat. Good thing you aren't.'

'Okay.'

'When he comes, just grab the back of his collar. He won't bite. He'll follow you if you keep hold of him.'

He nodded again. They went in opposite directions.

The music from the porch stopped at the same moment as the noise from the schoolyard died away.

She could hear the boy calling between the houses.

She had thought that when the end came, she would feel relief. Never again to lie awake (*You prepare a table before me in the presence of mine enemies*) listening for the wolf down the hall, not to barter with Bobby, trying to outsmart him before he could put her into one of those boxes.

Her husband died right in the pew, slumped to one side, the light from the stained glass flowing over him. In grace, the priest said, called to God's side. The priest told her that the light from the stained glass was how we understood God, but in heaven there would be only the pure light, no glass colouring how we saw. In heaven she would know God as God knew her.

She was so jealous. Her husband had cheated her of what should have been her death. He'd barely believed. She hadn't noticed he was dead at first because it was ordinary for him to fall asleep during Mass. He used to make fun of the priest, said he was a faggot. The boys would laugh along with him, imitating the priest's long pauses. She sat, fuming, got up to clear the plates. Dying, he'd taken something that should have been hers, that shaft of light, the drama of whispers through the church, the priest trailing off uncertainly, the paramedics on the lawn. He'd done it to her again, she thought, the way he'd fork up the last of the meat from the pan without asking.

Well, she couldn't have that death. But something like it, at least? Not lying at the bottom of the stairs with her dress wet, not so thirsty.

The yellow glass darkened, she imagined for a second it was Gabriel coming home. No, just the shadows growing. The pain was bad enough that she couldn't describe it, thinking of the doctor asking her to rate her pain, but this pain had no number, it seemed to come from outside her body, opening her like a hook, like a talon, a beak, like a wolf's tooth. Her dress with the large blue roses was barely damp now, the smell growing stale, she wished someone (God?) could see her, look, look, she was sitting up.

Felix called so his voice was almost breath. He wouldn't frighten the dog, he called in the gaps between the music from the porch and the schoolyard. Wait for it, hold on, go. Like finding his feet when he walked alone. He felt a great calm washing over him, the scream leaving his body. He knew what he had to do now. Put away everything else. His mother, the blood on Sylvie. Just do the job. He was finding his feet.

The shadows along the grass and bushes and parking signs were knives. He hid between the houses, his eyes adjusting to the darker space. He called. Watched for a lost shape, slow and old, nose dragging along the pavement.

When a dog sniffed the earth, the earth was a story. Dogs read smell like humans read words. That picture of how dogs see: faded, blurred like an old TV show, like a Polaroid floating in water. But that was wrong, trying to think your way into dog-seeing. You couldn't climb out of human-seeing into dog-seeing. You couldn't climb out of human smell into dog smell. He wished he could. Dog smell: the whole world singing.

He closed his eyes, trying to climb out. Each smell like a note, an explosion going off inside him. But he was still himself. Stuck inside himself. Warm pavement, new grass, something rotting. Garbage from in front of the empty house. A dead rat lying at the peak of the pile. He opened his eyes. A dog could pick out the parts of each smell like he could see the leaves on that tree, hard-edged with light, and the dog would never see that. Some people thought there were other worlds, and there were, right there, the dog was in another world, sealed off, he and the dog could stand side by side and be in different worlds.

Dogs saw ghosts. If you saw a dog stare at nothing, you could crouch and look between the dog's ears and you'd see the ghost too. He didn't want that. He wanted to be inside the dog's head, all the concrete and garbage and every living and dead thing divided into many parts, not just an armpit or a sewer or old meat, high notes, low notes, what felt smooth to him was actually sharp and ridged. Nat liked to say something about angels dancing on the head of a pin, that was smell for a dog, everything ordinary was full of angels dancing. All around him, out of reach. Dancing. The scream was gone now.

He'd read about ancient dog skeletons, they'd pulled loads thousands of years ago, grooves worn into their bones. Dogs followed humans into their caves, sat by their fires, walked beside them through their fields when they learned to farm, lay panting at their feet, looking up. A dog skeleton dug up from a fifteen-thousand-year-old grave in Germany, the family burial mound. Human bones, dog bones, mixed together. In the same world at last.

If he had a dog, when the dog looked up into his face it would be the same way dogs looked at humans a thousand years ago, ten thousand years, hoping, trusting. Did dogs know people lived in a different world? Were they sorry for humans, who smelled nothing, heard nothing?

When you looked at the stars, you looked at dead light. The stars were already dead, they were the past, above you was the past, the deep past, all around you. Every rock. And everything that was in the world has been in the world since the beginning of the world.

When a dog looked up at you, waiting to see what you would do, what you would give, what you wanted, that was the past too. Not the deep past. But the far past. Far enough.

He climbed a fence. The yard looked dark below him, the grass dark as water. In the breaks in the music he could hear the woman calling, *Ringo*.

He heard his own name shouted: Nat looking for him. He would not be found.

Find the dog, grab the collar in the spot behind his ears. Pull.

In her kitchen, Maddy hung up the dishtowel. She'd caught Milo covered in dust at the sink, throwing handfuls of water on his shirt. She stood over him while he washed his hands, singing 'Happy Birthday.' He ran upstairs to change without his usual foot-dragging. She wanted to call after him to take his clothes off in the bathtub, decided against it, thinking of her own mother, the too-clean apartment after the divorce, the rules about what could be eaten when, where shoes must go, connected to bouts of stifled weeping. She wouldn't manage Milo, she wouldn't pry. Milo could sift grit onto the carpet in his room, leave grey trails in the bathroom, reminding her of the trails rats left, smears of oil from their fur that showed the quickest way. Along the baseboard, behind the cupboard, the links from hiding place to hiding place.

The sun was lower. She couldn't see through the curtains of the old woman across the street who sometimes spied on Maddy. But Maddy's windows were so dirty from the dust drifting from the house next door, the old woman probably couldn't see anyway.

Why had she run after Nat? Stupid, stupid. She should have let her walk away and turn back, recalling the dinner, she should have deftly engineered a crisis, made Nat find Felix and force Felix to apologize, she would forgive Felix, and Nat would feel how admirable Maddy was. She'd wasted a chance to be stringently generous. Standing behind her daughter, holding her frail shoulders.

Upstairs, something smacked the wall in Sylvie's room. Maddy should call her down, examine her hand, ask her if she'd taken the money. Or maybe she wouldn't ask her, what Felix had done made it irrelevant. Sylvie was so timid. Blameless.

Maddy, her second year as a theatre student, shy at a party she'd come to with an older man she was half-heartedly dating (thinking back, he'd hadn't been so much older, but at twenty a few years felt vast). Nat standing in the middle of the crowded living room, arguing. Nat was a graduate student, the girlfriend of the woman whose house it was, not Frankie. Maddy didn't know Nat's name or the name of the man Nat was arguing with. Like the man she'd come with, they appeared fully adult, enviably sure. They were clearly friends, swaggering wide-legged and drunk, gesturing at each other with their bottles, dressed in almost identical uniforms of cargo pants and sweatshirts, the same short dyed hair, showing off to the room, an argument about Marxism using terms Maddy didn't know, and she felt the flare of purpose between the two speakers, the unstable pleasure they took in shouting at each other. She remembered for twenty years that feeling of standing with her back to the wall watching Nat, rebuked by the assurance of her opinions, the way she interrupted her own thought with a new thought, laughing, and by Nat's poise, her slovenly poses. Maddy was foolish, for the time she'd spent choosing her dress, straightening her hair, blending discreet makeup into her cheeks and nose. Nat looked at her and dismissed her, barely registering her presence. Maddy felt her own irrelevance and was ashamed, remembering that shame, years later on the street corner with their strollers, Clio and Sylvie studying each other, the sense of being assumed to be trivial, as if Nat wasn't preoccupied with the same problems as Maddy, the same unwieldy failure to be appropriately satisfied. Nat couldn't hide that she hadn't remembered meeting Maddy at that party. Sometimes Maddy was irritated that Nat thought she couldn't tell that Nat only pretended to remember her, when Maddy's life had been spent studying small hesitations, shifts of expression, interpreting the minor tensions and betrayals that exist within daily exchanges. Nat didn't notice what Maddy saw.

Nat came home. She couldn't find Felix. She picked up her phone from the counter. Nothing from Frankie. She texted: *When will you be home?*

Frankie must have been waiting for her. *I'm sorry about this morning. I love you.*

Come home soon. There was a weird thing with Clio and Sylvie. I can't find Felix.

What happened?

Come home soon

Dots, disappearing. Frankie staring at her screen, trying to achieve the right tone. Finally: *Don't worry. I love you.*

Nat, who thought love was beside the point for the moment and who hated being told not to worry, didn't answer. She imagined Frankie rushing to her bike, wanting to protect Nat from her fears, to protect Felix from Nat's fears, Nat wanting to protect him from Frankie's insistence that all was well. Frankie had even written her thesis on Julian of Norwich. *And all shall be well, and all manner of things shall be well.* But Nat couldn't believe this. The same impasse, repeated endlessly. That was marriage. Wasn't it?

Was Clio upstairs? Should she call her down? She took the components of a salad out of the fridge, lined them ready on the counter. The kitchen shone. She stood in her kitchen, wavering at the sight of the new tile, the sink, the glass jars of oil and vinegar, the kale in the bowl.

The men on the porch seemed to have turned down their music, and she could hear the brass band practising in the schoolyard, some effort at good cheer that she would not participate in. She'd remembered something at the school, flyers, invitations to donate costumes.

Nat rarely thought of that party where she must have met Maddy. She remembered the man she'd argued with, though she didn't know him anymore. And a fight with Frankie later, after Nat told her girlfriend she was tired and caught up with Frankie at the corner, both so overwrought with secrecy that a fight was inevitable. Nat had dropped the bottle, half flung it, the broken glass vaulting upward, the street light, almost morning. They were in the middle of their affair, less secret than they thought; in retrospect, Nat assumed many people must have known, or guessed. Yet she remembered the secrecy as so exciting she couldn't breathe, she thought her heart would stop. But thinking of that time, she pictured herself as a different person, a stranger.

The woman she'd betrayed had later married a man who was a film editor; she lived with him on the Sunshine Coast and posted pictures of large panting dogs, Nat thought she worked for a dog rescue or maybe just owned a lot of dogs. Easier than children, more biddable. You knew what a dog wanted and could give it.

If she'd thought about that night, considering herself standing in the centre of the room, almost dancing with the force of her own argument, in relation to Maddy, brushing her hands against the wall behind her, in her blue velvet dress, Nat might have said it was sociologically interesting, each now in a kitchen, foiled. She might have added something sententious and general about women, and then she would have stopped herself and said something reflexive about privilege, and she would have sincerely meant both statements but would have, underneath, experienced a sharp pain like heartbreak, thinking of both of them at the party, the force of their expectations, their sense of difference from one another and from what they'd come from, heartbreak as if something essential had been missed, as if she'd wasted an enormous amount of time.

She did not know what this essential thing was, only that she had missed it. That spark of herself, standing arguing. If she was honest, she would have conceded that part of her sense of her own magnitude had rested in being half-aware as she spoke that someone was watching her, hovering by the wall in her blue dress, someone who had meticulously prepared herself to be there and was stuck on the edges of things, that Nat needed an observer to watch her and admire her and not know what to say.

Maddy left her phone on the kitchen table, pretending she would leave it behind when she went to Nat's, knowing she would not. It was too late, but her agent kept odd hours. She sometimes stalked her agent a bit. Wondered if she was an alcoholic, noting her posts across her various platforms got stranger as the day dwindled, incoherently belligerent around midnight.

In bed Maddy glared at her phone, not turning on the light if Alex was asleep beside her; they both kept up a pretense that he kept her from sleeping, but usually she was the one who lay awake, scrolling. His breath untroubled. If only they were obviously troubled with one another, obviously unkind, a story she could tell when women found themselves swapping stories, trying to gauge what was reasonable from the reaction. *No sex for eight months. He refuses to be home when my family comes over. He texts a ball-and-chain emoji when I ask him to stop at the grocery store. He told our daughter she couldn't wear a miniskirt.* Something that could call forth a pause, a look around the table: no, that's not normal. He was enviously normal. She sometimes checked his search histories, but nothing. When they had sex, a passable amount for a long-married couple, she took a certain pride in her own performance. She didn't know if Alex thought of her when she wasn't there.

The man working next door had left. She'd heard his truck starting, rounding the corner, where Alex rounded the corner on his bike in the morning without noticing she had come out of the house. She would have waved to him if he'd looked back. It was his fault for not looking back. She'd been ready to smile like she loved him. Did he think of her? She hoped she meant Alex and knew she meant the young man in his truck. She wanted someone to think of her. There was nothing on her phone.

Nat didn't remember meeting Maddy at the party but did remember her from a few years later. A friend had made Nat come with him to a warehouse to see what he'd described as a deconstructed *Three Sisters*; his boyfriend was the lighting designer. Nat was living with Frankie then, settling into her own future. They were talking about children in a misty romantic way, a far-off possibility. She didn't want to go to the play.

The warehouse was cold and smelled of paint and stale cloth, the smell coming from huge swaths of red fabric hanging from steel girders. The scant audience sat in a square of chairs, and the actors rose up before them in the dark, appeared from the folds of red fabric, setting it swinging, they ran barefoot in the aisles between the chairs and stood, turning to address all four sides of the spectators, stepping between pools of pale blue radiance to speak to each other. Nat read in her program notes that the director wanted to return Chekhov to his primal earthiness, rescue him from a history that saw him as a restrained and realistic playwright. The actors roared and laughed garishly and sobbed like clowns. Loud bangs. She looked at the floor.

And then there was Maddy, playing Irina. While the other actors hurled themselves across the space, she was still. As the play progressed, Nat understood she was watching something remarkable. This young woman held nothing back, but so unobtrusively you could almost miss it. She was above the indiscriminate histrionics around her. She didn't press. In the scene where Irina agrees to marry a good man she doesn't love, who knows she doesn't love him, she stood in the centre of the stage, smiling minimally. He stopped talking. Without looking at him, she slowly removed all her clothes, dropping them on the floor behind her. The audience watched in concealed embarrassment, telling themselves this was commendable, a sign of their cutting-edge sensibilities. Nat was shocked, watching Maddy's face. She thought she was seeing a person's soul, more clearly than was possible in life, offered without vanity or any instinct for self-preservation. Maddy stood shivering under the cool stream of light, greenish and smooth like a mysterious object glimpsed underwater, and Nat wept because Maddy didn't. She just stood, knowing she was giving herself away, knowing the man would never have her love and that happiness was not coming, no matter how worthy she was. She was more than the too-literal false note of her nakedness; she was a different kind of nakedness, willing to give up every illusion, as if it were possible to do that without dying. At the end of the play, Nat huddled stricken in her chair, thinking of Maddy's face when she imagined going to Moscow, how her voice was almost breath, not meaning anyone to overhear when she said, *But it all turned out to be nonsense. Nonsense.*

When she saw Maddy in the baby group, she remembered her face but didn't say. She wasn't used to meeting actors and didn't want to embarrass Maddy. Later, she didn't say because she wanted to keep the memory private, finding Maddy as she was in life trivial, not free of vanity at all.

Nat wasn't sure she could describe seeing Maddy onstage without ruining the image in her head, warping it into this shallowly discontented woman who needed to be told constantly that she was admired, who lapped praise like a small child spinning in a favourite dress. She couldn't reconcile the two Maddys, wondering if Maddy onstage was the real Maddy, not spoiled or silly, a person of bravery and fine feeling, a vessel for the beauty and tragedy of the world, giving herself away as a painting or a song or a poem does. Somewhere inside herself, Maddy was capable of that, and it changed who Maddy was. Nat had seen that secret. She wanted to keep it for herself.

She would change her clothes, Maddy thought, looking down at herself, she should change before they went. Alex would be home soon. She'd put on a dress, earrings. Nothing was finished. There was a long streak of something chalky down the front of her shirt, probably sugar, but it looked like plaster dust from the house next door, sifting through her walls.

Felix didn't come home.

Nat thought of how she should describe all this to Frankie, what she would say, but the more she thought about it, the more inconsequential it seemed, as if she'd preemptively taken on Frankie's reassurances. Of course Felix was mistaken, of course he hadn't meant to hurt Sylvie, of course he would come home. He sometimes walked for hours, and this time was no different. There was nothing to do but wait. It wasn't dark yet.

Nat could hear Clio in her room, playing that Ed Sheeran song she and Sylvie were obsessed with, a fit of longing for childhood before it was over. She pictured Clio sitting cross-legged on her bed, the song an assertion of her innocence. (That was good, wasn't it? If she wanted to feel innocent, she must be capable of feeling guilty?) Even annoyed by the repetition behind the closed bedroom door, Nat remembered missing what she had but was about to lose, or missing the sanitized version of it, the longing for what had never existed. Maddy liked to reminisce about playing Emily in *Our Town* just after graduating, and Nat (who wondered why she never mentioned *Three Sisters*) struggled not to tell her that the play pandered to the audience's desire for a kind of belonging that did not exist outside of fantasy. Thornton Wilder had no home, a bullied bespectacled boy barely surviving his peripatetic childhood, unable to join anything, growing into a man carrying himself with a dignity that lent itself to being jeered at. His most significant relationship a tattoo artist and pornographer who Wilder, older, proper, must have loved against his will, his love for this man inseparable from humiliation.

She looked at the clock. Frankie should be home by now.

No Felix.

She massaged the kale, looked up eagerly for Felix at the opening door. Frankie caught her look and she kept it up, smiling as Frankie stumbled over all the shoes and boots, carried the bike pannier into the kitchen and set it on the floor. Nat wiped her hands, the kale leaving a dry film.

Frankie stopped just before she reached Nat, testing. 'I'm sorry.'

'Me too.'

Frankie kissed her. 'Okay, we did that, so tell me what happened.'

Nat had to explain who the bird woman was, and Frankie pretended to remember, and Nat allowed it. The point was Felix, his accusation, his rage, his headlong run across the street. Frankie turned away, lifting glasses from the shelf above the sink (this was the ritual, the drink after coming home). She listened attentively, yet still doing all the things she would do on a routine evening, and Nat, who'd expected to be irritated, was moved, as if Frankie, in the practised gestures, was telling her all would be well without pressing, without insisting. Only showing.

Nat wondered if this patience (with her fears, her dissatisfactions) would go on, or if there would be an end point, when Frankie would announce she was finished, perhaps after the children were gone?

'Let's do a shot, babe.'

It wasn't Scotch, it was tequila. Nat laughed.

'Come on. Why not? Get through the evening.'

'Sure. Yeah. Why not.'

Frankie slid out another cutting board beside the one Nat was using, sliced wedges of lemon, licked the juice off her hands. 'I promise he'll be home soon. And if he isn't, I'll go look for him.'

'Okay.'

Frankie kissed her neck.

She turned back to the salad automatically.

'You smell good,' Frankie said.

'I showered. Lucky you.'

'Lucky me.' Frankie kissed her again.

Nat couldn't think of anything else to say, but she was grateful as Frankie, in mock exhaustion, rested her head against Nat's shoulder blades. She took the weight of Frankie's head.

'Come on. Drink.'

They knocked back, both exaggerating their expressions, and Frankie turned Nat to face her. The tequila tasted clean and lively. They kissed purposefully, Frankie steering her toward the opposite counter, hoisting her up onto it. Sliding her hands under Nat's shirt. Nat tilted her head back, letting the day and her upset wash over her and turn into sex, something she was good at. She wanted to cry and could transform that into coming quickly, her legs wrapped around Frankie's waist, before anyone arrived. It would be the sufficient addendum to the apology, an extension of it (but she pushed that thought away, it was dreary, as if her whole life was instrumental). Frankie got to Nat's zipper, but then Clio clattered downstairs and that was that. It was enough, Nat thought, jumping down from the counter. It would see them through being on one another's side for the evening.

Clio entered cautiously. They both frowned at her, and Clio, resigned to a lecture, sighed, shrugged, offering to set the table as a deferral, which they accepted. Frankie adjusted the dimmer, got candles from the sideboard, napkins. They stood side by side, folding. Clio was up to Frankie's shoulder, when had that happened? Frankie showed Clio how to make a cocked hat, a leftover from her waitressing days, that French place (did it still exist?) where everything seemed to melt onto the plates in pools of yellow sauce. Nat, waiting for her to get off shift, sitting at the bar nursing a sullen red drink and her sense of superiority to the moneyed middle-aged diners, armour against feeling out of place in her frayed sweater and leaking winter boots. Frankie, hair in a bun just before she cut it off for good and quit the job, harsh white shirt, touching the back of Nat's neck as she passed. Nat shifting very slightly on the stool, Frankie knew what it meant, lifted her hand, turned to a table, and brought the bill, smiling to herself. Nat didn't know if straight couples felt this secret thing, or if they were already so public that it was not the same. No one, casually looking over, would have that momentary confusion, not sure what they saw. Though that didn't really happen anymore. Everything was public now.

Nat could see Frankie trying to time her moment right, pursing her mouth, watching Clio as she folded, Clio at first anxious about being asked to give an account of herself (she must know that Nat had told Frankie about the day) and then letting herself think she could get off scot-free. That was childhood's ability to shrug off the past, make it truly past. It was only later that it caught you. Clio's head bent to the task, forgetting. About to be ambushed by Frankie's well-intentioned insistence on timing, which suddenly seemed too powerful, the tyranny of adults arbitrating the world. Nat wished someone (Maddy? The teacher at that meeting about the girl who told them, without directly saying so, that Clio was cruel, even if the principal didn't think so?) could see how Clio watched Frankie's hands, glancing at her face for approval, shaking out the napkin over and over until she got it right, then artlessly pleased, holding it up for Nat to see it resting on her palms like a wounded bird. The calculation that Nat sometimes caught in Clio's smile smoothed out into genuine innocence. She didn't want to talk to her; she wished she could tell Frankie through a look. *Yes, you're right. I give in. Let it go.*

'Nat! I did it!'

Nat aimed a kiss at Clio's head, Clio snaked away, protecting the napkin.

The kitchen and living room were separated by a granite-topped counter. They had knocked the wall out in the renovation. The room softened in the candlelight. The red tulips bought yesterday by Frankie from the corner store with the black buckets of cheap flowers at the front door stood waxy in the glass vase, set in the centre of the table. The stems turning pink, then white further down, showing where they had met the earth. Frankie had dropped a few pennies into the water so the tulips could feed on the copper; she kept a container of obsolete pennies in a kitchen drawer for that purpose.

The table was right. The room was right. *And all shall be well, and all manner of things shall be well.* Glancing up from the salad at the lights and candles and flowers, the glasses for water and wine, the place cards Clio was now writing for fun (there was a stack of cards and a pen kept in the same drawer as the pennies, Frankie liked organizing), with little flowers drawn beside each name.

Where was Felix?

Frankie was right to have persuaded her to rip out the first floor of the house, to pore over paint chips and samples of flooring, a year of tense consultations about lines of credit. They had arrived in their settled lives: the grey-and-blue rug that echoed the blue walls, the soporific beeswax candles with their squat flames, the low sun through the window above the sink, in the backyard flashing spears of green coming up from the bulbs they'd planted in the fall, the raised beds surrounded by a fur of early grass. The children, older, no longer trampled it.

They had gone to a photographer friend of Frankie's and small black-and-white portraits hung on either side of the kitchen window, framed in polished wood. Clio on the left, Felix on the right. Felix disliked being photographed, but the man had caught his friendliest face, his eyebrows drawn together as though he was trying to remember something. Clio had put on a string of plastic pearls, borrowed from Sylvie; she was still close to dress-up, to dolls with their sleepy complacent smiles and teased plastic hair. Clio's smile imitative, wistful, her lips pressed, the pearls cinched tight around her throat, trying out an idea of herself. She wanted to be mysterious and alone. Maybe she was young enough that she thought of herself as Cinderella. Not the cartoon princess winking at talking birds but that book Nat used to read her with the slightly sinister woodcuts,

Cinderella poised at the top of the stairs, composed in her sad beauty, everyone looking up.

And that Hansel and Gretel, like a medieval book of hours. Five-year-old Felix taking the book into his lap, explaining to her that he'd figured out something. The witch and the mother were the same person: look. *No, no, no, no,* Nat insisted, he was mistaken. They just wore the same high cloth headdresses. He turned away. He wouldn't be shaken in what he knew. The world was full of witches for him.

Nat looked forward to when the photographs would inevitably be spattered with grease, sticky dust gathering along the top of the frames. Broken in, broken down, there had to be something worn and provisional for a room to feel real.

Frankie watched Clio with the place cards, Clio frowning in concentration, Frankie frowning too, trying to figure out the most appropriate moment, flummoxed by Clio's self-possession.

The room gleamed. The oil coating the dark leaves in the salad bowl gleamed.

The marching band grew nearer.

'What the hell?' Frankie asked.

'Remember? The community band Hannah was trying to organize with the kids?'

Frankie nodded, pretending.

'Don't you remember? I know I mentioned it.'

'Should we have joined?'

'Well, since none of us know how to play any instruments and we all hate participation, I thought not.'

'I meant as a gesture.'

'I think they can manage without us.'

Frankie poured herself another shot, raised her eyebrows at Nat, who shook her head.

'I bought dessert.'

'What?'

‘From that place on Queen across from the bookstore, what’s it called? I bought macarons and a cake. It looks like a tiny wedding cake.’

Nat hadn’t noticed the white boxes that Frankie had slid out of the pannier, now resting on the sideboard, fastened with embossed gold stickers. Frankie, like a child, piqued that Nat hadn’t noticed.

‘But I told you to come straight home, I said I needed you to come home.’

‘I did.’

‘Not if you stopped at the bakery.’

‘I’m here. And he isn’t even home yet.’

‘Exactly.’

‘Are you mad at me?’

They both saw Clio’s shoulders lift, dropped their voices to conspiratorial mildness.

‘No. I just thought you’d come straight home. Like I asked.’

‘I ran in for five minutes. It was so sunny and I saw them in the window and I thought it would be a nice thing. I’m sorry you’re upset. It was really five minutes.’

They looked at each other bleakly. Nat, feeling unreasonable, changed tack. ‘I told you we didn’t need anything. Maddy is bringing dessert.’

‘So? We’ll have both.’

‘We can’t do that.’

‘Why not?’

Nat shrugged as if it was useless to explain. Frankie poured Nat the second shot she’d refused, nudged it toward her.

Nat didn’t pick it up. She’d said no and there was oil on her hands. ‘I don’t want to offend her.’

‘You said everything hurts her feelings no matter what you do. Anyway, the kids will love it, won’t they? More treats.’

‘She’ll make it into something. Like a thing I’ve done to make her feel she’s not useful.’

'How do you know?'

'Oh, she won't say. She'll just *look*. You know how she gets.'

This was safer, if they could retreat together into complaint about Maddy. Nat hoped Frankie would take the peace offering.

'Screw her then,' Frankie said obligingly, and Clio giggled. 'Oh honey, sorry, swearing jar. Forget I said that. That was bad.'

'I do love that bakery,' Nat said.

'You could have told me she was bringing dessert.'

'It didn't occur to me.'

'They won't be fresh tomorrow.'

'I'm sorry,' Nat said, wondering why on earth she was apologizing.

A silence, punctuated by the scrape of Frankie sliding the pastry boxes onto the top of the fridge, moving slowly, Nat thought, to underscore Nat's unreasonableness, the silence growing, and Nat didn't know how that happened, how two people could carry twenty years between them and yet not help falling into standoffs over things neither would remember.

The silence grew, and each considered whether to press or let go. Frankie sipped at the tequila meditatively. Clio watched. Nat wondered if that was marriage for other people too. She didn't know, that was the difficulty with happy marriages, they were not worth talking about, and so she couldn't know if everyone stood in their kitchens and found themselves staring at a gap they thought they'd successfully closed with a drink or an apology or an attempted fuck on the counter or whatever else was useful, a rag to stuff into the cracks in the walls. She assumed so; to think this was a unique experience would be ludicrous. She wondered about silences between Maddy and Alex, but that wasn't a fair comparison. They were desperate, even if Alex didn't know it. She perked up a bit, thinking of their desperation. She washed the oil off her fingers, glad for the sound of the tap.

'We can have cake for breakfast tomorrow!' Clio announced from her corner with her pens and cards.

Frankie decided. 'I would love that. You're a genius.'

Nat was grateful to Clio, dried her hands.

'I'm sorry, love,' Frankie said in her ear. 'I should have come straight home.'

'Can you go look for him now?'

'He'll be home soon. It's not dark.'

He was supposed to come home when it got dark, and they wanted to be more like their own parents, telling the kids to come home when the street lights came on. The orange flare in the dusk, the park changing in an instant, Nat walking the dog with her brother trailing after her, shivering. Their mother not yet home from work.

Sometimes Nat wondered if Frankie recognized some aspect of herself in Felix, some sadness of her own earlier years that she knew he wouldn't keep. Frankie recalled her childhood relatively uncomplicatedly, if distantly, like a restaurant in a faraway city in which she had once eaten a pleasant meal. She was not given to regret. Felix was all regret, and yet Nat wondered if there was something about sharing blood that made Frankie have faith in him.

Nat couldn't say this to anyone, certainly not Frankie, who would have been shocked and grieved. Nat thought it only furtively; it was too at odds with what she wanted to believe and knew to be practically true. She was there. Packing their lunches, listening to their teachers. It was a private terror, picturing herself shut out. There was no one to tell who would not be either appalled or confirmed in what they already believed, which was appalling. She rarely let herself think it. Frankie just assumed their luck would hold. Nat didn't know if this position was admirable or delusional.

She was about to ask Frankie again, when Frankie turned on Clio, setting down her glass to indicate her seriousness. Clio capped the pen and looked up. Another child, Nat thought, would have hidden in her task, pressing the nib down harder on the paper. She didn't know if this meant Clio was truthful or adept at appearing so. She didn't know if, later, she would find she'd made a terrible mistake, fretting over the wrong child.

'Did Sylvie do it?'

Clio shook her head. 'No.'

'Really?'

A pause, Clio considered. 'If she did, I didn't see it.'

'And your brother?'

'He attacked us. He just made it up. Then he *attacked* us.'

Frankie was about to speak, and Clio, realizing she'd gone too far, went on quickly.

'He made a mistake. You *know* he makes mistakes.'

Another pause. Clio kept her eyes trained on Frankie's, and Frankie gave up easily.

'Well, let him walk it off and come home hungry.'

Nat didn't want it to be that easy. 'I don't think this is done, Clio.'

Clio, vindicated, ignored Nat.

'We can talk about it more later,' said Frankie, who wouldn't.

'Could you go look for him now, actually? I really want you to.'

'They'll be here any minute, it would be rude.'

Nat picked up her glass and retreated. 'I had a weird conversation with Maddy about it.'

'Weird how?'

'Like I couldn't get her to talk to Sylvie, like at all, like because Felix lost his shit there couldn't be anything else going on, and then she asked if they were still coming tonight, like I was going to tell her not to come.'

'That's funny,' Frankie said, wanting Nat to find it funny. And all at once she did, the day rearranged.

Nat giggled. Not caring that Clio was listening, interested in the world of adult malice. 'I guess it was funny.'

'Everything's the big catharsis for her, isn't it?'

'Well, she's always ready for her close-up.'

'Where *are* they, anyway?'

'You're right, they're late. Ready for Alex to pretend you're one of the neighbourhood dads?'

Frankie, who didn't mind, made a face. It was a relief to be meanly united against other people, and they were laughing as the doorbell rang. Frankie touched the back of her neck as she went into the hall. Only the screen door was shut, and Nat called to them to come in, but they waited, the family group, smiling expectantly, Maddy and Alex on the top step, Sylvie and Milo standing on the sidewalk.

Maddy heard laughter through the screen door: Nat, backlit, moving unhurriedly, absorbed in a joke.

'Come *on*,' Alex muttered, at Nat or at Sylvie and Milo, who lolled below them against the fence.

They were late. There'd been no time to tell Alex anything that had happened; she couldn't think of where to start, and anyway, she thought, he wouldn't understand. Milo had to change his clothes. Sylvie had ignored her father's shouts up the stairs and come down slowly, wearing those plastic pearls Maddy hated, hiding her hurt hand. The pearls weren't meant for a child, and Maddy worried people might think it was her necklace that Sylvie had borrowed. Like she was a woman who would wear a string of plastic pearls. She couldn't say this aloud. Alex would frown at her. Alex, in his spring suit, damp from his bike ride home, no time to change or go for his evening run, exasperated at being kept waiting. She should touch his shoulder, something minutely wifely, reassurance and admonishment at once, but she didn't move. If she left him, would he think differently of every time she hadn't moved, hadn't answered? Or would it never make sense to him?

She touched his shoulder, as if she'd found a leaf or a twig. *I'm trying*, she thought, untruthfully. *No one can say I'm not trying.*

(Alex wearily mulled the case against the landlord, the tenants who might be put out on the street, which Maddy hadn't asked about.

He'd brought it up at breakfast, thinking she would remember, and she didn't acknowledge that he'd spoken. He should leave her alone to get over it, whatever it was, he should not be hurt by these things, he would not let himself be injured, he'd ceded the right to be hurt over daily omissions to her long ago. But he mentioned the case again in the hall when he got home, as his family shouted around him, reminding them of his day, and no one answered. He stood for a moment, in his sweaty clothes, wishing someone would answer, and Maddy stared at Sylvie, who looked down, something was happening and he didn't understand, why did Maddy think he wouldn't understand?)

Maddy saw Nat's house was cleaner than hers, had not yet lost the newness of replaced windows, unblemished walls. The sun was heavy between the alleys, the men on the porch across the street turned down their music and shuffled inside, and Nat swung open the door.

The light behind Nat met the low sunlight, and Maddy could not speak, even to apologize for being so late, when Nat, prompting, said, 'Well, here you are.'

Alex was waiting for her to apologize, it was Maddy's job to apologize, but she was dazzled, stepping inside the house.

In the distance, the woman called her dog over and over, but the band (should she have joined? Would it have been good for Milo?) blared out again, almost upon them, only one street over, Maddy thought, and that was all they could hear.

Passing through the hall and into the dining room, her eyes swimming, she recovered herself, exclaimed at the table, waved her hands dismissively when Nat took the tart and set it on the counter, praising the crust. The berries had darkened, curling at the edges. Nat, chilled from the scene on the sidewalk in front of Maddy's house, insisted there was nothing for her to do, and so Maddy stood, rubbing her right elbow with her left hand. She could hear Alex talking, asking Frankie immediately for an opinion and giving his own before she had time to answer.

The fridge was yanked open and slammed shut, Frankie handed out beer, stood beside the fridge with Alex, each adopting the hearty persona they'd cultivated in place of a friendship. Frankie did this with some irony, Nat knew; Maddy didn't know if Alex did and would not have cared.

Nat and Maddy stood at the counter, turning their backs on the stream of commiserations about family life, house maintenance, work, though their work had nothing in common and Maddy thought they barely comprehended what the other did. She didn't either. Frankie's work was administrative and well-paid, that was all she knew, and when she stopped to think about it, she could not picture Alex's days, only an important stream of long hours and apologetic texts. If he'd seemed hurt by it, she would have countered that he could not picture her days either. But he asked questions, he showed interest. She had no power to hurt him. Perhaps she had not tried to hurt him enough; she was saving it for a later time, saving it all up for when she would wreck her life, which she would not do, she would keep postponing it, gnawing at the possibility (she checked her phone, and Alex, seeing her, shook his head).

She tried to catch Nat's eye as Frankie and Alex laughed too loudly, wanting to show she was recovered from their conversation earlier, and the easiest way was sharing a twinge of embarrassment at the effort their spouses were putting forth, proving something. That they were the heads of households? That they were taking full advantage of their lives?

'I thought you didn't like beer?' Nat whispered.

'I don't,' Maddy whispered back, and Nat conspiratorially took it from her and poured her wine, hiding the beer behind a row of white canisters.

'Frankie gets these ideas. I don't know why. She doesn't like beer that much either.'

Maddy tried to think of something funny and disloyal to say, but Nat moved away, spoke into Frankie's ear, and Frankie shook her head. Maddy saw Nat's face collapse for a moment as she moved back to the sink, but perhaps she was laughing, a joke that would not be explained. She envied that Nat, whatever her irritations, appeared to share a series of private jokes with Frankie, pulled faces and small gestures. Alex was measured when he disapproved. Lawyerly. He did not condone exaggerated complaints. He reasoned out the other side.

Milo played with the tulips, creasing one of the leaves, a seam of darker green appearing at the fold. She should make him stop.

'Can you go look for him *now*?' Nat whispered to Frankie.

'He'll come back soon, love. Let him walk it out.'

Nat stood at the sink, blinking. Frankie was sliding open the glass doors, showing Alex the river stone they'd used for the patio. Nat should turn around. Maddy was watching her.

The girls ignored Milo, who had ruined one of the tulip leaves. They stood looking fixedly at each other, Sylvie with her hand at her throat, covering the ugly necklace of Maddy's she was wearing, then showing it to Clio in some kind of message. Clio examined it, began audibly counting the pearls. Nat did not like their hermetic games. But she did not believe that Clio was solely to blame for whatever was between them, something nasty. They didn't realize how regret worked; it could be years until one or the other stopped in their tracks, recalling things they'd done or said, knowing they could not escape themselves and no apology would be enough. She thought of the girl and the drawings, the meeting with the teacher.

Sylvie stood unbending as Clio touched each bead. Girls invented rituals at that age: Nat remembered getting her best friend to nick along her arm with a piece of glass, making patterns of her steps, crossing her fingers and toes in a particular order before she went up the final flight of stairs at her school, past the cupboard she rushed past after a classmate told her the ghost of a murdered boy lived in it, and she had not grown up to be more than usually compulsive. She'd just liked the rhythm of it, the rules governing her body, like the rhythm of a skipping rhyme, chanting words without really knowing what they meant.

O where are you going with your love-locks flowing
On the west wind blowing along this valley track?

Cutting her arm with a piece of glass.

The girls in the schoolyard. Their secret games.

Glass.

Christ.

She pushed this away, she couldn't manage the thought just now.

Where was Felix?

The counting went on, low.

The berries on the tart were liquefying in the sugar; if she'd been Maddy, she would have waited and brought them with her in a bag. She hoped Maddy didn't notice the white boxes on the fridge.

Maddy watched Clio count the beads. She finished, drew back. Sylvie relaxed. Two more years and they would go to different schools. Maddy would make sure, maybe send Sylvie to a progressive private school, where she didn't have to wear a uniform, though she'd look sweet in a grey blazer with an embroidered crest, and maybe they did take the coins, maybe they did terrorize that other girl who was so quiet, so bewildered, but it was Clio who thought of it, girls were vicious, Sylvie was not a girl the way Clio was, Sylvie was a child waiting for instructions. Maddy believed she could sense Sylvie's thoughts and Milo's, as if she were a membrane that enveloped her children so they were still attached to her. Sensing changes in the air, in the space around her, changes in their breath as they slept, dreamed.

She did not say things like that to Alex, who would have reminded her of Maddy's clinging mother, of how much Maddy didn't want to be like her mother. Maddy didn't mean that she thought her children had no right to a life separate from hers. In her mind this membrane was delicate, airy, nothing like the meat of a placenta or an umbilical cord. Threads of milk or blood in a cup of water. Sensitive as a sea creature, those pink and glowing white tendrils unfurling along the glass in the aquarium where they'd gone over March break. Sad because the ocean was dying, warming, or losing salt, she could never remember which would come first, acidifying, but she did not know what that was, only that it would kill everything. The dead oceans, which she pictured as miles of clouded water, stilled, a flat endless sheet of brown silt.

The girls ran upstairs, thumping.

Nat came up behind her, touched her sleeve the way she did, never touching skin.

'Are we okay?'

Maddy thought, *She really is my friend.* She must have believed Nat wasn't, to be so moved by *we*, as if they had a friendship separate from their children, separate from Alex and Frankie, who were back inside and talking about city politics and property taxes and renovations. They would never be friends. She and Nat were friends. They must be, or Nat would not have said *we*. Maddy was startled at how happy she was, overtaken by happiness.

'Yes. Yes. Sweetheart. Of course we are.'

'I wish I knew where Felix was.'

Maddy grasped her shoulders, shook her jokingly. 'He always comes back.'

Felix would come back, and however sad Sylvie seemed, Felix was more so. Maddy's child did not walk the neighbourhood alone, imitating, without meaning to, the man who lived with his mother and walked by himself, muttering, half-tolerated by the woman on the porch with her dog and the men across the street who drank all day. Maddy could afford to be generous.

'The house is so beautiful, Nat.'

'Isn't it? Frankie was right. I thought it was crazy to do all this now, but she was right.'

'Did you just say I was right?' Frankie called.

'Don't let it go to your head,' Nat said, not turning around, and Alex found this hilarious.

'I love the blue,' Maddy said, letting go of Nat's shoulders slowly. She looked up, craning her neck as if the ceiling were far above her. 'And the light. There's so much light now.'

She'd envied this house the way she envied Frankie and Nat's covert jokes, envied her younger self learning to imitate a walk, and thinking that she could do this all her life, that she would never be confined but would pass easily between many selves. Watching the row of prisms her mother, who wove inept wall hangings and collected antique glass bottles and was alone now in a small apartment, had hung in the kitchen window. Watching the broken pieces of sliced white light edged with red, yellow, blue crossing over into one another. She had thought she could live like that.

Nat looked tired, red-eyed. Maddy hoped Milo had washed his hands again when he changed his clothes. She resisted taking out her phone. She wanted to hug Nat, but Nat was not a person to be spontaneously hugged. Maddy stopped herself, wishing there was a way to show that in this moment she felt no envy of Nat or anyone. She did not need envy.

'Beautiful,' Maddy said again.

Dinner was a success, Nat found, surprised. They drank, not too much. Clio and Sylvie, contrite for what they had almost certainly done, told stories from school. Milo left the tulips alone when his father sharply told him to (Nat was pleased, wondering if Alex tried to correct Maddy's indulgence). The asparagus Frankie had steamed as an afterthought was perfect, the salad was praised, the pulled pork gleamed over the edges of the buns, left grease on their chins. They made fun of one another and admired the setting sun. They avoided tricky subjects: where Felix was, Maria or Marianna and her coins, the men on the porch, the boys in the schoolyard, and Nat thought they avoided these things out of a negligent affection for one another, knowing they would not agree. Right then, that was fine with her, as she looked at her guests and her kitchen. It did not matter who agreed and with whom, given the material similarity of their lives. If she paused, afflicted, setting down her coffee cup, her house strange to her, her life strange to her, how could she know that Alex, when alone, did not feel alien to himself? She couldn't imagine it (he was trying unsuccessfully to pick a tendril of meat from his teeth), but that was her failure, not his.

She reached across the table to pour Maddy more white wine, and the wine caught the light, opulent as honey, twisting from the bottle into the glass. She looked at her own wrist (she liked her wrists) and the stream of wine and Maddy's face, a little flushed, and felt a burst of significance like a flashbulb going off, she would remember this, whatever happened after, the light and the wine pouring in the light, it would become part of what she thought of as her past, one of those rare times when she was unambiguously happy and knew it. She didn't know why she was happy.

She put worry for Felix out of her mind the way she put aside the possibilities of Clio and Sylvie and broken glass. She forgot him. Later, she recalls this with a shame so great she can't tell anyone, not even Frankie, when they sit up in bed trying to make sense of the night.

She'd read an essay in graduate school by a philosopher about a painter, which she'd hoped, in her early enthusiasm, to relate to poetry, because this seemed an arena where the main point was to draw nebulous lines between things that otherwise did not match.

The philosopher, discussing the work of the painter, described it as a tension between the human desire for something to happen and the terror that nothing will happen, which the philosopher related to the Holocaust. The abstract painter the essay considered employed bars of colour like doors about to swing open into white space, into nothing. The viewer looks and simultaneously experiences the sublimity of something happening alongside the other sublime, the horror of nothing happening. Nothing ever again. Nat had remembered this, thinking that she was afraid that nothing would happen again, not in the cataclysmic way he, and perhaps also the painter, meant, but in the most trivial sense: time will unwind itself blankly. And then, arriving without warning, this. Looking across the table at familiar faces and knowing something is happening.

She remembered Felix. It was only a moment, her forgetting, but it doesn't help her later on.

Maddy sliced into the tart. Slivers for the adults, larger wedges for the children. Milo picked his up in his hands, scattering crumbs. The tart was good, not too sweet. The crust held. It did not matter about the softened berries. Milo demanded ice cream and was shushed by his father. Frankie offered coffee. Nat got up.

'I can do it, love,' Frankie said.

'I'm going to look for him.'

'We have guests.'

'But – '

'It's fine.'

Frankie, shaking her head, lifted the coffee down from the shelf. Nat sat down.

Alex looked at his plate, and Maddy wished he had looked at her, that they could note together the small hostility, the faults that appeared gratifyingly in other people's lives. How much she wanted to see that the people around her, who seemed so sure, were tiptoeing resentfully around an edge. It was unworthy, to want that suppressed dismay (Nat pulled her chair hard into the table), but she would have liked Alex to look at her.

It was forgivable to not be sure whether she loved him or had ever loved him if she never said. It was forgivable if it stayed a secret.

After she left Alex, she would tell the story of that night and place her decision later. She told the story sincerely; she believed that, in the shouted instructions and the useless beams of flashlights and cellphones, in the sirens growing nearer, as the people in the street, stepping back as the police cars arrived, became spectators washed in blue and red lights, she decided.

She couldn't resist the structure: realizing with the force of a blow to the jaw that she couldn't stay, because the least she could do, the very least (and she brought her hand to her chest, pressing her heart, her voice rising, not noticing how close she was to the woman in the café), was live authentically, having seen firsthand how transitory we are, how easily torn away. Of course, that was the moment when she understood she must change her life.

But really, she was just frightened and not sure what was happening until after it had happened. She made her decision now, watching Alex sip his coffee and compliment Frankie on the beans.

It was the clarity of thinking she must keep her secret that made her, underneath, know she would not, even if she forgot and placed her revelation at the crisis. It was permissible to realize she couldn't stay if this was wrung out of her reluctantly, not her fault. She wanted her choice to be inevitable. Not looking at him across the table (he tried again to pick the string of meat from his teeth) and admitting she was finished.

Nat almost got up again, didn't.

Milo, swallowing his tart, began to sing. Softly, not interrupting the conversation. Crumbs around his plate. Hands clasped, imitating something he'd seen, a singer, a child on a greeting card.

His voice, Nat had to admit, was sweet. He hit the notes, and more than that, as he sang, his hands loosened as if he were no longer following his own movements on an imagined screen. Nat could see he loved the faraway cartoon hills, Belle striding toward the vanishing point in the landscape. She'd read (googling idly, bored on the couch next to her children when they were younger, watching *Beauty and the Beast* over and over) that the yellow dress Belle wore later was a nod to Cocteau's film, and she was pleased, thinking of the cartoonists studying Cocteau and wanting that more complicated, more ambivalent image, a reference that only a few people would notice, right there in the centre of the story like a piece of ivory set unexpectedly in a plastic bracelet. Thinking of this, she disliked Milo less.

Maddy smiling, stroking the hair at the back of Milo's neck, Alex raising his voice to drown Milo out. Nat saw Alex could hardly bear it, his son's caressing intonation, his wife's mawkishness. They should both leave Milo alone. She should leave Felix alone. She wanted Felix to come home.

'That's enough now,' Alex said, and Maddy laid her palm on Milo's head, shushing him or siding with him against Alex, it wasn't clear to Nat which. Alex picked up his fork.

'Very nice, Milo,' Frankie said, and Milo beamed at her. Sylvie and Clio snorted, making faces at each other.

Nat half rose, sat down again.

When Nat thinks of this afterwards, she is angry with Frankie and with herself, so angry that she takes to walking late at night when Frankie has at last fallen asleep, moving quickly along the streets near her house. It feels like swimming, like a swell under her, borne along between the street lights. There's a short darkness between the lamps, a few feet of shadow, and she passes through it and thinks of the light and the dark as water.

As she walks, she pictures herself at the table, standing and going past Frankie, outside where it's not fully dark yet, ignoring Frankie calling after her, ignoring her guests, ignoring her other child, in her mind she runs down the front stairs and along the centre of the street.

Ten minutes earlier.

She walks between the street lights.

Ten minutes.

As Alex sets down his coffee, they hear the band, in the schoolyard or the next street, growing louder, growing closer, and the adults make a joke of it, what jerks they are that they didn't join, they feel they are above community bands and brass instruments, though they don't want to be, they like the idea, they want these things to exist even as they themselves are too embarrassed, too busy, but the din is part of what makes the neighbourhood special. Everyone is by now a little tipsy, just enough to feel each moment, that the evening is full of evidence that they are living exemplary lives.

Maddy, looking at Alex, thinks there is nothing wrong with him and for the first time that day means it, though she has decided. She is gone and doesn't know it yet.

The music lurches toward them, and they see through the window that the players are passing in front of the house, dressed, as Nat imagined, in loud cheerful costumes, everyone out of step, people with their children, some of the children delighted and some glowering, hoping not to be recognized. The procession reminds Nat of the Portuguese dancers at the street festival every year, in their peasant costumes, the children and teenagers who are forced to learn the dances as their parents learned them, though it is several generations since anyone wore these clothes or executed these steps without the self-consciousness of cultural preservation. Of course, this band is not the same people: these are the members of the school's parent council and the neighbourhood association and the committee that organizes the communal garage sale each spring, and the dancers and committee members do not know one another, they maintain a benign indifference mixed with soppiness, at least from the committee members, who think the dancing is wonderful. Nat does not know what the dancers think; she doesn't know them.

It is dark enough now that she and Maddy and Alex and Frankie and their children (where was Felix?) are framed in the window, a picture of an enjoyable dinner winding down, and she doesn't get up to look for Felix, it would be too conspicuous to walk out of her house while the band is marching by, she will wait a little longer.

Clio rescues the last crumbs from her plate.

The band passes and the street is quiet.

Clio privately believes for the rest of her life that she heard the woman calling her dog, and then Felix calling too, underneath the shouts of the woman, but she couldn't have heard clearly enough to know who was shouting, or why. She only thinks she heard her brother. That he asked for help. If she'd paid attention, she could have heard him.

She licks her fingers clean.

She was sitting up. The pain was dull, she realized. It must have blunted over the hours (she could see the clock), partly tamped down by hunger. She rolled up her smelly dry dress and examined the map of her skin. When the boys learned to walk, she'd see a look on their faces sometimes, thinking someone would notice what they were doing, thinking everything must stop because they could balance. Move away from the walls and chairs into the middle of rooms. The overjoyed shock on their faces. She refused to make a fuss. Old, from her window, she'd seen the woman across the street watching her children stagger along the sidewalk, the way she'd clapped for them, told them they were wonderful, that she couldn't believe it. Was that what a mother was supposed to be? She'd looked over from the stove, seen them doing this thing, and gone back to her work. Even with Gabriel, who the doctor said might not walk, she couldn't remember that flushed incredulity when he did, what the woman seemed to feel. Didn't the woman know there was no need for so much noise? But sitting up, she felt the same expression on her face as Gabriel, as Bobby. She looked around, testing her neck. Fighting the sense that there was no one to see, not God either. Just the house, and a house sees nothing. She was sitting up.

Ilya was almost home. There was his building, the driveway to the small parking lot. He pulled into his space. His phone open on the passenger seat, another of his father's lordly emails asking for money. He'd sent four emails when Ilya didn't answer the first one.

Lisa had thrown his father out, of course. Maybe this was it. Maybe no woman would put up with him again. Ilya didn't want that. His father would be his problem.

He could see his window, mired with leaves, between two recycling bins. He liked the way the sun struck the window as it set. This was the right time. He would sit, watching the light catch the glass, watch it turn from gold to pink to grey, the same elation as watching the embers of a cigarette scatter along the pavement, come to rest, burn away, always missing the moment when the spark crossed from being into not-being, collapsing into brittle ash. Some reprieve from the burden of himself, peaceful coherence with the world, like lying in the tent long ago and looking up at the branches laced against the moon.

Turning off the truck, he settled, leaned his head against the seat. Thought of the woman, the way she startled slightly when she saw him. A lulling thought, like the cigarette ash, the branches at night, like the possibility of sleep.

Something would not loosen, and it was not the emails (he reached for his phone, drew his hand back, not wanting to answer), it was not the vision of the woman. It was her son, the boy in his cape, it was the plywood cover, the water.

He did not move, he should get out of the truck, shower, eat a sandwich, he should watch a movie and try to sleep, he should answer his father, he should answer the emails from the lawyer, from the wives, he should sleep, he could sleep now.

He turned his head from the window, he could sleep in his truck, it would be a warm night, he didn't want to move, his eyelids were so heavy, his eyes hurt, but there was the red cape with the gold lining, the boy's face, his plans, so secret he didn't know them himself, he would only know what his plan was when he had done it, Ilya remembered that, plans undertaken too fast for second thoughts, fast as thought, faster. *Think first,* his mother screamed (the bloody hand, the broken window), *think first,* but she did not understand that that was not the point, the point was giving in to something faster than thought, something that came before it, that was childhood, he'd seen it in the boy's face and he was afraid, it would not let him fall asleep, the boy's face was Ilya's problem, it had to be someone's problem, he turned the key, cursing the boy and himself, he backed out of the driveway.

A splash.

He is following a scent, he follows it down into the darkness. Everything is dark for him now, blotched with absences. He noses at the smell, leaning further in, his paws testing the edge, then crouching, liking the cool shadows, the earth, and everywhere, everywhere, rats. He remembers digging holes, lying guarding the holes, his muzzle resting in the humid dark. He doesn't have the energy to dig anymore, but the hole is already there, so large, so full of smells. Then the earth gives way under his front paws, he scrambles down, lands heavily, buckling.

The water, while not deep, is rising, soaking his feathered fur. He barks at the rats, blindly hopeful. They retire unhurriedly into their holes. He works his tongue over the fibres of rope snagged in his teeth, sniffs the water all around him, the water dims the scent but can't cover all of it, the unfurling of this place: plaster, clay, concrete, metal, brick dust, rat shit and piss, the raw smell of scraped and hacked roots of trees.

His hind legs shake, cataracts cover his eyes, he has growths behind his left ear and at the base of his tail, he has scratched away some of the fur on his back and the skin shows in fledgling-pink wrinkled patches, but smell is still magnificent, he trusts it, he staggers in circles, following his hunches, the smells lead nowhere, yet he doesn't despair, he is sure this sense will show him a way out.

If he kept crossing, back and forth (weaving, like he was a spider setting a trap), Nat wouldn't find him.

Then he'd lost her.

Slower, he looked into backyards, the walkways between houses, between and under parked cars.

Nothing. He couldn't go home. No one believed in his innocence. He'd done only what was necessary.

How late could he stay out, if the dog was nowhere?

He dragged his feet for home.

Wait. Wait.

Splashing, whimpering. The lights were off at Maddy's, so no Milo, fucking Milo. *What are you doing? Felix! Felix, what are you doing? Watch me. Watch me!* He hated that kid.

Whimpering.

He knelt. Something sharp on the pavement. Don't think about it. Pain was nothing.

It wasn't dark yet, but he could feel the dark coming. And the hole in front of him was darker than the night would be. Someone had moved the plywood cover, pushed it up against the pile of garbage.

The beam from his phone showed only water.

But the water churned, moved by a living thing.

Ringo, he whispered. *Ringo, Ringo.*

Don't scare the dog. It might not be the dog. It might be rats. Maddy talked about rats all the time with Nat, loudly like they should have an audience.

His shoulders were through the hole. He'd never really thought about where the hole went. Into the basement, a drop down into water. The light shone along the basement walls, rows of eyes like metal, shrinking back into the cracks.

A rat could fit itself into an opening the size of a quarter. That dead rat beside the pile of leaves. Faded fur, dried gut like dark red twine. Some of the bones broken, splayed open. So delicate they looked hollow, bird bones.

Rats were as old as dinosaurs, older than people. Everything was older than people. Everyone wanted to talk about people, what people did, what they thought, what they meant, what they would do next. People were nothing, people were insects who didn't know they only had one day. Look at a timeline: ancient time, deep time. Humans the dot at the end, almost not-there. No one should think about them.

He had seven missed calls from Nat. He could call her and tell her about the dog. She would run down the street, take charge of Ringo, of him. She'd figure out getting Ringo out of the basement. She wouldn't ask him for help.

He would do this on his own. She would know he could do something on his own. No one thought he could do anything.

The dog struggled forward. He reached out his other hand, the dog snuffled away, out of sight. The water was up to the dog's knees.

Ringo, Ringo.

Felix looked back at the porch, where Clio and Sylvie had cut the rope because they were bitches and liars. The porch would fall over soon. Lawn ornaments lined below the front window, perched between the black metal railing. Gnomes, plastic green-and-blue birds, flashing silver-and-pink pinwheels.

The front yard was packed dirt, with a birdbath he'd seen the dog drink from. Figures circled it, animals and humans cast in blobby chipped terracotta. Algae slicked the bottom. Dogs weren't fussy about water.

In the reddish light the birdbath looked like an altar, the figures were part of a ceremony, not dollar-store stuff, they were watching the water, serious and holy, something was about to happen. A song, a sacrifice. Like those pictures of Stonehenge, like the knives at the museum, useless under glass.

The main ambition of his parents was that nothing should ever happen, they wanted to protect him from the catastrophe of something happening.

Sometimes when he was alone he saw it, a flicker in the corner of his eye, the world about to reveal another plane, the lawn ornaments becoming druids. He wanted to hear that music. He could almost hear it. Almost climb out of himself.

Humans the checkmark at the end, but he liked thinking about older times, sacrifices to gods, stone knives, humans brushing against what was not them, they looked backwards over their shoulders like the bird woman, knowing how little the world cared for them.

If he rescued the dog by himself, that would be something he had made happen.

The rats were something. So was the long note of the woman with her coins and her screech, when she screamed about her father and Yugoslavia, he didn't know what Yugoslavia was.

Nat never wanted to know why, she only wanted to be sorry or angry, she did not notice what was important in the song of the woman, the man in the alley, the dog in the water, the rats.

But the rats were gone. The pump had stopped. Water streamed from the cracks in the front basement wall. He could hear it.

He called again, more loudly. He could not scare the dog away; there was nowhere for the dog to go. Wet fur matted, in a far corner, wanting his back to the wall.

Felix told him not to be afraid.

The dog barked once, bowed.

He hooked his ankle around the sawn-off end of a metal bar, left over from the chain-link fence. He tugged at it with his foot. It would hold.

He slid his phone into his pocket. The dog was scared of the glare. Leaning further, he willed the dog to come forward into the one patch of fading light below the hole.

The dog moved, fording through the water.

Maybe he could touch the dog's head if he reached down. He was almost there.

There was the shadow of Gabriel at the door, darkening the bubbled yellow glass, glowing from the last of the sun. She must get up. She'd thought she'd hear him come up the stairs, but there was music from somewhere, uneven music trying to sound like the military parades of her childhood, her father in his badly fitting conscript uniform. Parading up and down the square.

The music quieted slowly, like the marching band was moving away, and she braced herself against the wall, braced herself for the fumble of his key, but then she heard a truck skid, half-covering the sound of something falling into water. Gabriel shouted. She thought the old dog had been hit by the truck, she shut her eyes against the terrible whimper, *Holy Mary mother of God pray for us now and at the hour of our death,* but the prayer made it worse. Gabriel was shouting. She must open the door. She didn't know if he needed help or if she must prevent him from doing whatever he was doing, the worst thing, it was happening at last. She must open the door.

She was standing. One hand spread against the wall, she found the light switch.

The hall sprang up. The faintly sticky wood floor, the pressboard mahogany sideboard, the white-and-gold clock under the plastic dome. Earlier she'd thought these might be the last things she saw, and now they weren't. But she wasn't able to open the door. It was the worst thing.

Gabriel's voice. Another voice. A sound she didn't recognize. It was happening, and it didn't matter that she couldn't bear to open the door, that the pain in her side had woken again, as bad as the first moment after she fell, nothing mattered except that she open the door, to prevent, to help, she had the door open now, she fumbled her way down the stairs, the truck was in the way of seeing anything, voices low to the ground. She must walk around the truck. She could hear water.

In his sister's boathouse, Ilya made lists. He had no self left, only a collection of softened damp scraps he carried around in his pocket, covered with writing he couldn't read. He made lists of things to remember.

At first he wrote them on his phone, then stopped because the phone itself, the world streaming out of it like a flow of blood that couldn't be staunched, came to seem like part of what threatened to make him into a pile of torn paper. He would go over his lists in his head. He couldn't yet comfortably hold a pen, and his writing cramped and wavered, the writing of a young boy waiting to be told he can stop.

On the list, the camping trip when he was ten. His stepfather, insisting they were now a family and this was a thing families did, drove them to a campground near Guelph, pointed out the excellence of the site he had chosen, set back from the gravel, a creek running behind it, dappled with light through the cedars. He nudged Ilya's mother for praise, but Ilya knew it was dumb luck, picking out a number on a map of a place he'd never been.

The air above the creek was thick with insects. Ilya didn't know if they knew they had only this one day. Ellie sat on a rock, waving her hands around her ears, refusing to help unpack, rubbing her ankles together to ease imaginary mosquito bites. Ilya whispered that they would be attacked by wolves and she hissed *Fuck off.*

Behind them, her father sweated over the tents and his mother refused to complain.

He scrambled down the bank and across the creek, slithering from stone to stone, soaking his sneakers. The insects parted their clouds to let him pass.

Moss on the stones and pebbles tumbled in the water and white sparks of quartz, he filled the pockets of his jeans, oblong wet patches at each hip and down his thighs. A trove of beer cans caught in a weave of slippery brown branches flashed silver and red. He was up the bank on the far side, pretending not to hear his mother calling.

After the tents were set up, his mother organized the food, and his sister, scowling, changed into her bathing suit. He could see her blundering inside the tiny green tent. They all walked down the path, nodding at other families, past the bathrooms and the public taps, past a flimsy playground, down to the beach full of people and geese. The geese hissed, raising their heads from the sand, which was garlanded with their green-and-white shit. It floated in the shallow water, haloed in murk.

Mothers pulled at their children, and the smallest dug trenches to make the water flow from the lake. He watched the lake dribble along the furrows and then surge, crumbling the sides and bubbling brown in the holes. He found an abandoned hole and thrust his foot down. The water was warm. The beach smelled like sewage. His mother and stepfather set up the chairs they had carried and sat. Their chairs were orange-and-yellow nylon, leaving red welts along their thighs when they stood up.

Ellie ran into the water, forging out past the shit and the buckets and shovels and the toddlers borne up by their plastic armbands. She swam toward a cliff on the far side of the lake. Turquoise bathing suit, tanned limbs cutting a path, her hair streaming behind her, and she was freer with every stroke. Free of the garbage and the geese and the burning children and her father and his mother.

In the tent the moon was so bright he could see every shadow branched above him, echoing the pattern of sunlight he'd seen when he'd waded into the water, a linkage on the sand below, moving, and the branches above him moving, like the world was fractals, overlapping, spreading out. Even Ellie, drawn as far away from him as possible and cramped between her air mattress and the fabric of the tent, was part of the pattern.

He realized he could hear the highway. The cars, sliding through the dark, closer, receding.

He could picture the cars, the long approach of their headlights glowing in the trees before the curve, sweeping over him like search beams, passing him unseeing, along to the other curve, the light fading, the roar dwindling, rhythmic as waves on an empty beach, a beach at night, the water curving up to the shore, the sand ridged by wind, no footprints. He could picture the cars so clearly he must have dreamed them, or seen them in a movie, he was never sure.

Cursing, he ran out of his truck as the boy (but not the boy he expected) slipped through the hole. The light didn't reach far enough.

'Are you okay?'

His phone was in the truck. Closer, he could see the boy struggling, sitting up in the water, hugging his knees.

'Can you reach my hand?'

The boy didn't move. Behind him another shape, soaking, stooped, fuck, two children in the basement, but this one was wrong, this one was badly hurt, misshapen, no, fuck, not a child, the old dog, shaking himself with the deranged cheerfulness of dogs, nuzzling the boy, who grasped the dog's head.

'Can you stand up? You have to stand up.'

Ilya waited. The boy was whispering into the dog's cocked ear.

'You have to *stand up*.'

Ilya looked over his shoulder for help, and there was the walking man in the middle of the street, examining the truck's open door, and Ilya took this to mean help and jumped into the hole. Realizing as he did that this was foolish. Too late, he was in now, his hands scraped where he'd braced himself against the masonry. *Think first. Think first.* But here he was.

The water was halfway to his knees. He could see the broken sump pump, tangled with a piece of chain. The dog's eyes and the boy's eyes watching him with the same passive stare, relieved that they were his problem. They didn't know he was not capable of rescuing anyone. They must not find out. Ilya would be worthy of their stupid trust.

He turned back. He could get his hands over the edge of the hole. If he heaved himself up, he could reach down and help the boy scramble out. Or get the boy to lift up the dog to him? Or was it better to try to climb up at the back wall where the stairs used to be and find the ladder? But then how would the dog get out? He didn't know. He was useless.

The water was not rising very fast, but the light was going.

He thought he could hear two people talking in front of his truck.

'Can you get a flashlight?' he called, and they fell silent, stunned by his voice.

'My phone was in my pocket and I think it smashed,' the boy said finally, and then: 'I'm sorry.'

'We can climb out,' Ilya said, so convincingly that the boy stood up.

'My name is Ilya.'

'I'm Felix. This is Ringo.'

The boy, incongruously remembering what he'd been taught, offered his hand, and Ilya took it as the dog shook again, the drops flying into Ilya's smiling mouth, tasting of clay, his smile needless, the sun was behind him, nearly gone.

The water was very cold. Felix and the dog were calm. Perhaps they didn't believe this was actually happening.

The voices again, one urging the other, steps going and a door opening. More silence and then a light, not the glare of a phone but the yellow beam of an old flashlight. The dog backed away, gave one short sharp bark.

She told Gabriel to get the flashlight from the drawer by the sink. He moved heavily, he moved the way she felt, pain ribboning through her. Soon she must sit down, right there in the street, she would sit down and howl, as if she were the wolf and not Gabriel (was that true?). She shouted at him to move faster. Didn't he know there were people, the boy and the young man and the old dog? And there he was with the flashlight, and she saw he knew this was his chance, his one chance to do something right, and he knelt at the hole and she wished his brother could see him, not his brother, someone else, she thought of God but she didn't mean God, God saw anyhow, she must not think like that, as if God didn't know, but someone. Maybe herself but as someone else, the person she should have been, who had never been afraid of him and wished she could leave him in his glass box, she wished to see him in his rightness as God did, and he leaned down, wedged the flashlight between two bricks. She could sit, but the ground looked far away, the asphalt rippled like dark water, if she sat she could not get up again. They would carry her away. She would not give in. *You prepare a table before me in the presence of mine enemies.* Back straight, her frown clamping down on the sound she had in her throat.

Ilya saw Felix's leg was bleeding. A seam opened along his thigh, shining in the musty light.

'There was a piece of metal. It's over there.' He pointed to a floating brown shingle, a jagged strip of the aluminum siding they'd torn off the front of the house.

Ilya examined the jagged cut, and the boy shivered, not looking down at his own leg, Ilya's attention making him understand he was in pain. That the cut was deeper than it seemed at first.

At the top of the street, Nat left the door open behind her, leaving Frankie and their guests at the table.

The evening was warmer than she'd expected. In the fading light, the new leaves looked silver. She could hear the band, further away, looping back to the schoolyard.

The cars approached along the highway, Ilya could hear them and then see them, like lanterns swinging in the darkness, growing, swooping down on him, panic that they would not stop. They would run him down. Yet at the last minute he was saved, he was always saved, the car followed the road and curved, the lights receded. That must be the pattern of the universe for him, that he would be saved, that the cars would curve away from him, that he would grip the rope. The point of the memory that was a dream or a movie he saw once, that he would be saved, if only at the last minute, if only with his hands torn to strips, and the screams of the men, and the women sitting on either side of him in the lawyer's office, the wives with their naked faces, he would be saved but he would be accused.

The man reached down, and Ilya put his hand on the boy's shoulder.

'I'll lift you,' he said. 'And he can pull you.'

Felix shook his head. 'Ringo first.'

The front wall was swollen, water streaming over the masonry, seeping from inside the wall, between the bricks and the earth, the bricks shifting like loosened teeth under the onslaught of the buried creek and the digging and the spring. The rats watched.

The dog sniffs. The rats are watching him, though they aren't afraid of him. He is old and will be dead soon and he is not a pack animal anymore, his life runs alongside human life, theirs does as well but only provisionally, they were here before, they will be here after, they have time and time is on their side. They are an ancient civilization, contemptuous of more recent developments. They notice everything and are interested in what is practical for their own continuance and they have no wider curiosity.

Their river comes in faster and faster through the wall. Their memory of the house is older than anything else living. They tell stories about the house. The house is resigned to them, they know every path through it, and the house curves around them and accommodates them as if the people who have lived here and the ones who will live here in the future are only brief tenants. The rats know themselves to be the owners, the inheritors.

The dog barks again, but they don't move.

Maddy left the dinner table and followed Nat into the street, and they saw that the truck was stopped in the middle of the road.

They ran, not speaking, to where the walking man knelt, hauling something up, and the woman, coming back to see if her dog had made it home on his own, appeared at the curve, but she was slower, her knees stiff, and they arrived at the same time, watched by the old woman from the house opposite, who steadied herself with one hand against the truck's open door as if she might fall over. Something slimy and dark like a leech was coming up out of the hole. Maddy grabbed her phone from her back pocket.

She thought it was a monstrous child, and that was terrible, but it was the dog, soaking, wriggling, and the woman was on her knees beside the man, grabbing at her dog's fur, and the dog was lifted out and into the street, and that was when she and Nat, the light from Maddy's phone shining in the gap where the dog had been, realized that Felix was in the basement, Felix and the young man. Felix was bleeding but smiling, trying to reassure Nat, who screamed, pushing the walking man out of the way as if she couldn't bear for him to touch her son.

'He's fine,' the young man called up from the hole.

'He's bleeding,' Nat said.

'I'm *fine*,' Felix said, his voice loud to show his mother she was wrong. 'I'm *fine*.'

'I'm giving him a boost,' the young man said, 'and you lift him.'

Nat crouched, cutting her knees on something, maybe glass, scattered around the opening. She could hear the young man instructing Felix, showing him footholds. Felix's head appeared and disappeared as he bent to look at where the man pointed, the cracks in the masonry, missing bricks.

Time seemed very slow, and the two figures in the hole pedantic in examining the wall, she was supernumerary, too anxious, too much a woman after all, not comprehending the importance of their task.

They muttered to each other, pointing, and she thought Felix enjoyed this, underneath the shock of the dirty water, the blood along his leg. Given something difficult to do at last. All he'd wanted was to navigate difficulty, not to have the way smoothed out.

She reached down. He reached up. The skin of his arms looked grey, and she wasn't sure if this was because of the greenish light or a film from the water. There were a lot of lights; she realized there was an audience standing behind her. Springing up in the darkness. The sun was gone.

The old woman, her son, the dog, the woman on her knees speaking into the dog's ear the way Nat had spoken to her children when they were small, Maddy and Alex, Frankie, her hands clenched to keep herself from shouldering Nat aside, knowing Nat wanted to be the one to lift Felix out. Frankie was so good, in the middle of everything Nat was bowled over by the certainty of Frankie's goodness, and by how rarely she noticed it. Clio and Sylvie standing apart, and beyond them, Milo, his cape hanging limp over his shoulders. And the men on the porch, shouting encouragement, trying to offer assistance. They must have heard the noise and come.

When Nat recalls this later, she is rebuked in her second-guessing, her incisive politics and careful demarcations: here is this familiar group of people, growing in her mind to include the neighbourhood band, casting their instruments aside, and the woman who owns the café, standing aloofly in one of her exquisite linen dresses, and the people in the library with their smelly bags, and Maria or Marianna singing on the corner. Everyone is here. Not able to help but wanting to. This fantasy of everyone standing and watching her consoles her as she moves late at night between the street lights.

Maddy's phone whirs and she holds her hand steady, pointing the beam at the hole, but she still sees who it is and knows she wouldn't call this late if it wasn't good news and she takes this news as a sign that everything will be different. She will let her nails grow ragged for the close-ups.

Things will not be as different as she'd hoped, though she manages. Alex is scrupulous and fair and baffled. She has broken his heart, which she thought was impossible. When she realizes she has done this, she has to put it away from her. It's too much, to think of him, she needs to keep her eye on the future, in which nothing is finished, in which it is not too late.

Alex is brokenhearted, but in a few years he marries a younger colleague, a woman who doesn't want children and is kind to his. She loves Sylvie especially, and this is a blessing in Sylvie's life. When Sylvie leaves home, she texts her stepmother pictures: her room, her roommate, her impressive mid-term marks, dressing for a party. Her stepmother, who is very diplomatic, makes sure to imply to Maddy (she coordinates schedules, she manages Alex's life alongside her own work) that Sylvie tells her nothing. They commiserate about this, how Sylvie tells them nothing.

Maddy's basement-apartment windows leak in the heavier rain. She is often alone. When alone, especially at night, she sometimes thinks of the young man and what, if she'd been braver, she's pretty sure could have happened between them, and this becomes a talisman, as much as when, married to Alex, her brilliant younger self was a talisman. Because she won't see the young man again, she thinks of him more and more, and he becomes less like her memory of him as he was, transforms into another image of something she should have got and missed.

She sits in cafés with her phone, wanting something else to happen, she doesn't know what, hoping for good fortune beyond anything she can reasonably expect, and she doesn't see she is growing querulous and needy, that someone watching her might take her as a warning, like the woman in the café, who doesn't know she is a warning either.

She and Nat are friendly, but they see each other much less; the girls have gone to different schools, made other friends. Nat is a little constrained around Maddy, as if apologizing for her own ongoing marriage, which (Frankie knows, and Nat usually knows) has been fundamentally very happy. Maddy chooses to interpret this constraint as Nat's involuntary longing for Maddy's new freedom. Maddy makes jokes about this. Nat lets her joke; it would be unkind not to.

Nat is not envious. She is warned against amorphous, badly defined hankering after an unimpeded life. This is helpful; it curbs her resentments. She sees herself as a joke more, without seeing herself as having failed. It's immensely liberating to see oneself as a joke. She is less given to pronouncements. When the weird jazz dribbles out of the radio, she turns it off. Ruin is everywhere. But there's no point in looking for it. She knows that now, no longer in theory. It will find you anyhow, and you cannot hide or hasten.

She goes back to reading the poetry she'd intended to write about and sees less dread in it, more exuberance. This feels like part of aging, to stop fretting about the inescapable, though to say this would sound like a platitude, and she's trying to give those up. Or at least to give up thinking that if she hits on the right theory about the world, she will cheat death. Giving up unconsciously thinking this feels like a reconciliation with time, and with the dead people she's spent her life mulling over. She laughs at herself, saying to Frankie that thinking you can outwit death is a modern preoccupation except in fairytales (*tell the fish I want to be God*), and Frankie leans her head between Nat's shoulder blades and thinks Nat is making another theory, but is too peaceable to say this aloud. Anyway, they are planning a vacation to Spain for Clio's graduation present, and she's wondering about the flights.

Milo watches the people crowded around the hole and does not connect anything to himself. This is understandable at seven, but he never does, as an adult he doesn't look back on that day and think he might have been the cause of any of it. He is not given to introspection. This will serve him well.

Sylvie holds Clio's hand and Clio is overwhelmed with love and shame, shaking as she watches Nat reach for Felix, terrified for him, terrified by her love for him, because she is in fact perfectly decent, as Sylvie is, as the rest of the watchers are, as most people are, and both girls grow up to be relatively decent, not vicious, that was just something they tried on for a little while. The memory of her shame will stay with Clio always. It helps to make her decent: it reminds her to be careful, to pay attention, the way she might attend to a small stone lodged in her shoe, a manageable yet sharp pain as she walks. She doesn't run away and lie alone on beaches or have a mysteriously important job. She's a devoted daughter, marries young, the son of a childhood friend of Frankie's, they live in an apartment just across the bridge because of course they can't dream of buying a house without leaving the city and they don't want to. She finds she loves everything she thought she wanted to leave behind. On Saturdays, Frankie and Nat prepare elaborate brunches and Clio pushes the stroller over the bridge and tells her two-year-old, in whose face she sees the face of her brother, about her own memories of walking these streets, and the boy babbles, reaching.

Clio's grip hurts Sylvie along the cut from the glass and she hears the last notes of the band and remembers the bird woman's aria, the coins under the bed. For the rest of Sylvie's life, there's a small scar along her palm that she tends to avoid looking at. A line, fine as a hair.

Nat grasps Felix's arms at the elbow, he tenses, finding a space for his foot, the young man pushing and Nat pulling and Felix is out on the ground and the quiet broken, a surge forward, tugging him up and away from the pile of garbage, Frankie on her knees, examining the blood, and Frankie says she will get the car and take him to the hospital, and Felix is abashed, loved.

One of the men offers to get his truck and drive them, and Frankie, surprised, says no, no, that's all right, and he asks again, wanting to do something, and Nat sees he is sober, either snapped out of it quickly through years of built-up tolerance or (is she actually wrong about everything?) he only had a couple of beers over the course of the day, just a sunny afternoon at the beginning of May with some music, no harm, never harm, it's the younger man with the scar along the side of his face, and when he asks again, Frankie says yes, thank you, and Nat bites her tongue, lets herself be wrong, remembering Frankie's goodness and the possibility of his, and he points to his truck, says he works security at Saint Joe's, they know him in the ER, he'll get Felix seen fast.

There's a dark streak on Felix's cheek, his hair wet and slick, like the water was oil. His eyes are red, and Nat knows it's from whatever was in the water, but he looks like he's been crying.

Nat will find herself (on her night walks) thinking of him crying in the basement, alone in the dark and the water, though he was never alone, the dog was there, and so soon after, the young man, and when Nat goes walking by herself at night, part of what she carries is horror at herself, that she thought only of Felix, and the horror is so great she can't say it aloud, but she keeps thinking of Felix trapped in the basement and how she'd been eating and talking and not knowing. Sometimes on these walks she makes a leaning motion, the motion of lifting, thinking how she lifted Felix out and turned away, how she did wrong, not immediately turning back, as if there was a moment she could trace her way to and think, *That was where I did wrong*, though it's more a general intimation of the failure to notice other lives, she knows it's impossible to pinpoint an exact failure.

Felix escapes with a long scar like a piece of snarled white thread and a new reason for his sadness, but something happens to him because of it, he goes forward, he goes outward. This escape concentrates his life, though he would not have put it that way, but it's evident from the outside. He becomes singularly focused. He leaves, but with an intensity of purpose that they must love.

He comes home when he can. He remains very private; Frankie and Nat never hear much about a partner, or even his friends or the almost unimaginable details of his work. Clio does. To everyone's surprise, they are close as adults. He writes her long rambling texts, which she sometimes reads in the middle of the night, the soft whirr from her phone waking her up. His messages arrive at odd hours because of the time difference. She has a special notification for him, because she knows what he writes will make her laugh.

When they are old and he is a grown man, Nat and Frankie talk about Felix's dangerous work, and Nat thinks of him and the motion of lifting someone out of a hole and restoring them to their life, how Felix performs, over and over, the motion of lifting, amidst rubble and snapping wires and the smell of burning, the trapped people reaching up as he reaches down, how he wants to be the one who doesn't turn away from catastrophe because the sufferers are strangers to him, who doesn't draw a line between his life and other lives. Nat knows how rare this is. She's never managed it. She swims between the street lights.

That summer he walks the woman's dog for her sometimes, and sits on her porch, talking. She smokes while they talk, drinks beer, and Nat decides to ignore this, and doesn't ask Felix what they talk about. Later, visiting his parents and his sister when he's in the city, he goes to see the woman, he brings a case of beer, and later still, when she struggles to take care of herself, groceries, and when she's dying, Clio writes to let him know. He arrives a week earlier than he'd planned, he goes to the hospital and sits by her bed, telling jokes in case she can hear him.

In the fall he goes to a new school and finally makes friends, gangling or heavy boys in badly fitting clothes, who shut themselves up in his room. He never wears shorts so he will not have to explain the scar. But often, before he goes to school, he kisses the top of Nat's head as she sits with her coffee and she can hardly bear her relief, how glad she is, as if the young man, whose name, she now knows, is Ilya, was exchanged for her son's life, and in her secret self that is the only thing she really wants, that is the reason for her guilt, a word that means debt, a debt she owes to Ilya, but there is no way to pay it.

She tries to, clumsily, she talks to his family, encourages his mother and his sister (who she doesn't like) in a lawsuit against the owner of the house that drags on and goes nowhere; Ilya was not actually working, he was acting on his own behalf, and he'd already been involved in another accident, there was a pattern, yet Nat persists after the sister and mother stop trying, Nat phones the owner and tells him he is to blame, and whether or not he is to blame (he hangs up on her, blocks her calls, he is sorry but he is ruined, the house stands empty), she blames him so she might be free of her unworkable debt. She rants to Frankie about the man, the house, she keeps calling, and Frankie asks her gently, *Don't you know it's not possible to change anyone's mind?*

The old woman finally lets herself sit down in the street. She never tells anyone about lying on the floor all day. In the confusion no one notices that she smells, and she hobbles back inside as the police take witness statements, she successfully hides the bruises all along her body. Sitting in the middle of the road, she looks at the boy and thinks of her son, his key in the door, the box he was kept in as a baby in the hospital, his translucent skin like the skin of an egg, how he talks to himself, how there was going to be a terrible thing that was her fault, but she was wrong, her son wasn't a wolf after all. She wants to tell these people that she knows what it is like to love someone and be afraid of them and be mistaken, she knows this as well as they do, but they are talking too fast, they are not interested.

They turned from the hole to gather around Felix, the light sweeping over Ilya's face and away, as if he wasn't there at all. So many voices talking at once, like a party in another room. In the dark he could hear the water that was the sound of the cars bearing down on him along the road. The noise was almost reassuring. He experienced no particular urgency. The night was warm. Now the beams of light were gone, he could see sky through the hole, the first faint stars.

He knew he must climb up. He felt his way forward, the loose bricks and the earth and something like a tree root pressing up against his hands, and no one looked at him. He could hoist himself easily, it was nothing. Lonely, yes, that no one asked him if he needed help, and they would have, in another minute they would have. He couldn't blame them. But he was lonely.

Something was wrong with the wall. He couldn't get a purchase; it moved under his grip, heaving. It was alive, the way the sound of the cars or the fractals of moonlight above him in the tent were alive, or the screams of the men as they fell. He couldn't do anything. Even as he understood what was happening, it wasn't real. Or if it was real, he couldn't help it. The distance between him and the street increased, the sky wavered, the way a landscape seen through smoke wavers. He thought, *I must get out,* but he couldn't move quickly enough, like those nightmares where you must run and you don't run, where you must speak and your mouth won't open. As if he had to choose something and didn't know how to anymore, if he ever had. There was just dark.

They all turned back when they heard the sound. Falling. The wall came away in his hands, he cried out then but he didn't believe it, the wall was so solid, so heavy, yet it peeled away easily and came down on top of him, bricks, mortar, mud, the slew of water pouring in from the place between the wall and the earth, and it covered him, he didn't believe it, he couldn't believe it, they tried to reach him but it covered him down there in the water. Drowning doesn't take very long, they told each other later, repeating what one of the paramedics had said. It was nobody's fault.

Everyone there will, for the rest of their lives and at unexpected times (doing the dishes, picking up a child from school, running to catch a bus as the doors fold shut, stopping to notice an angle of light through trees), find themselves (painfully at first, but this fades) inside Ilya, becoming him as he looks up, seeing their faces at the hole, uncomprehending, shouting, growing less, growing further away as he goes wherever he is going, the wall is still falling and the water is still rising, but these things are beyond his concern, he's gone.

Acknowledgements

Thank you to the Canada Council for the Arts, the Ontario Arts Council, and the Toronto Arts Council, for support while I wrote.

Thank you to everyone at Coach House for all your work and enthusiasm and patience. Thank you especially to Alana Wilcox, for being a brilliant and generous guide, as well as fantastic to talk to.

Thank you, Kelvin Kong, for taking on this interior and slow-burning book, and for your unfailing cheerfulness and kindness and good sense and good jokes.

Thank you to Rachael Cayley and Mitch Davis, for loaning me their house while I finished the final draft.

Thank you, Adam Sol, for permission to quote from *Broken Dawn Blessings* and for some great conversations.

Quotations in the text are from Christina Rossetti, Anton Chekhov, Gus Kahn, Julian of Norwich, Gerard Manley Hopkins, Anne Sexton, and Psalm 23:5.

For reading and commenting on early drafts or parts of drafts, or talking me through small writing conundrums, thank you, Lea Ambros, Martha Baillie, Lucy Cant, Degan Davis, Bronwyn Fischer, Sarah Henstra, Brooke Lockyer, Jessica Moore, Alayna Munce, Catriona Wright, and Katie Zdybel.

Thank you to Denise Santillan and Kilby Smith-McGregor, for your good eyes.

Thank you, Peter Wills, for making sure I have a website.

Thank you to my family and to all friends and neighbours.

Thank you to my children: Livia, Tom, Danny.

Thank you to Lea Ambros, for what changes and what goes on. You're the point.

Kate Cayley has previously published two short story collections and three collections of poetry, and her plays have been produced in Canada, the U.S., and the U.K.. She has won the Trillium Book Award, the Mitchell Prize for Poetry, and an O. Henry Prize, and been a finalist for the Governor General's Award for Fiction, among other awards. Her writing has appeared in *Best Canadian Stories* and *Best Canadian Poetry*. She lives in Toronto with her family.

Typeset in Arno and Aukio.

Printed at the Coach House on bpNichol Lane in Toronto, Ontario, on Zephyr Antique Laid paper, which was manufactured, acid-free, in Saint-Jérôme, Quebec, from second-growth forests. This book was printed with vegetable-based ink on a 1973 Heidelberg KORD offset litho press. Its pages were folded on a Baumfolder, gathered by hand, bound on a Sulby Auto-Minabinda, and trimmed on a Polar single-knife cutter.

Coach House is located in Toronto, which is on the traditional territory of many nations, including the Mississaugas of the Credit, the Anishnabeg, the Chippewa, the Haudenosaunee, and the Wendat peoples, and is now home to many diverse First Nations, Inuit, and Métis peoples. We acknowledge that Toronto is covered by Treaty 13 with the Mississaugas of the Credit. We are grateful to live and work on this land.

Edited by Alana Wilcox
Cover design by Ingrid Paulson
Interior design by Crystal Sikma
Author photo by Livia Ambros

Coach House Books
80 bpNichol Lane
Toronto ON M5S 3J4
Canada

mail@chbooks.com
www.chbooks.com